To Nic

HAPPY BIRTHDAY

1996

Love Mum & Dad.

Maurice Shadbolt

Born in New Zealand of English, Irish, Welsh and Australian convict
ancestry, Maurice Shadbolt is the author of four books of stories,
several works of non-fiction and ten novels, including some now seen
as New Zealand classics. His most recent novel *The House of Strife* was
the third in a trilogy which began with *Season of the Jew*, winner of
the Wattie Book Award in 1987 and selected by the literary editors of
The New York Times as one of the best books of 1987. It was followed
soon after by the much applauded *Monday's Warriors* (1990).

'A magnificent writer' *Newsweek*

'Dramatically original' *The Washington Post*

'A master storyteller' *Los Angeles Times*

We hope this book will
• encourage you to put your
        feet up and
• take life easier
• keep you in touch with N.Z.
• be a good read.
        Lots of Love M & B

This Summer's Dolphin

MAURICE
SHADBOLT

This Summer's Dolphin

HODDER MOA BECKETT

© 1969, 1995 Maurice Shadbolt

First published 1969
Cassell & Company Ltd
England

This corrected and revised edition first published in 1995
by Hodder Moa Beckett Publishers Limited
a member of the Hodder Headline Group
46 View Road, Glenfield, Auckland, New Zealand

ISBN 0-34059957-X

Cover and text design by Dexter Fry

Printed in Hong Kong

For Daniel and Tui

Once it chanced that I stood in the very abutment of a rainbow's arch, which filled the lower stratum of the atmosphere, tingeing the grass and leaves around, and dazzling me as if I had looked through coloured crystal. It was a lake of rainbow light, in which, for a short while, I lived like a dolphin.

Thoreau

ONE

The island has a history of sorts, though its geography is more decisive. Seven miles of sheltered sea separate it from the mainland.

The Polynesians claimed it first, along with the rest of the country. Likely they warred over it. Many hills of the hilly island were once fortified, as sheep-grazed terraces show. But the clay of the island—boggy in winter, brittle in summer—holds slender record of that occupation and strife.

Some explorers missed charting the island altogether. They ascribed its contours, its bays and headlands, to the mainland. And the Maoris—or so they named themselves with the advent of explorer, whaler and then missionary—could not have set great store by the place themselves. For they abandoned it almost with first sight of European settlers gathering on near-by mainland. True, for a time they merely sold vegetables, taken by canoe across to the untidily growing settlement. But soon they, or most of them, evacuated the island to the first buyer. Probably they shifted to the town, or its outskirts; it is not clear what really became of them. Grog, disease? They merged with the town and vanished.

With them passed most myth and memory. The hills, where carved palisades crumbled, echoed with axe. That first buyer wanted the place only for its timber. That too went into the town—or city now—and when the island was ransacked from shore to summit he departed with padded pockets to parts unknown. But before he left he managed a sale, to a hopeful farmer.

So came the fires. They blazed for most of five summers. From the growing city on the mainland the island might have been seen, out on the bright water of the gulf, as a smoking and blackened hulk. The fire which had once shaped the volcanic island in earth's convulsion, given it form upon void, now returned it to aboriginal shape. Ridges and hills which once bristled with growth now stood clean, if charred, against the sky. And green returned, with pale grass among the ashes, in this strange and second spring. For never had a spring been quieter; the birds had been incinerated with the forest.

Sheep grazed for fifty years, and there is not a great deal more to be said. Across the water the city rose taller.

A little bush returned here and there, taking hold in gullies and inaccessible corners. Other parts of the island lurched, slumped, and finally washed down to the sea; the sea around was brown with mud in a rainy winter. Some of the island, more through contempt than despair, was given back to scrub. Farmers and farmhouses multiplied. One holding became half a dozen, then a dozen. Traces of gold, copper and manganese brought miners briefly from the mainland. The settlement they made died within a year. The island, in fact, had nothing in payable quantity. Nothing? There was the land itself, of course, as there had been from the beginning. The land; and across the water the expanding city. The connection was only a matter of time.

Geography? An island really has no sides. But since Motutangi is longer than it is wide it may be allowed, for argument's sake, two sides. There is the city side and the ocean side.

It is almost as simple as that, almost.

The ocean side is surf-beaten. There are high cliffs, black rocks, pale crescent beaches. In places there is still something of the wild. Pohutukawa tangle down to the waterline, trailing their fantastic roots in the sea, dripping their red blossoms into the surf. At noon the sea can be implausibly blue. A dreamer could awaken in summer shade on that shore and believe the Pacific still innocent of man.

The city side is indented and untidy. There are muddy beaches heaped with shells and dead sea-grass. Cans and empty bottles float in upon the tide, which then retreats across vast mud-flats. The tidal creeks are choked with mangrove and the haunt of flatfish and stingray. From here the horizon is confined by densely settled mainland.

The two sides, the two faces of Motutangi.

The second invasion of the island (if one concedes, that is, that those first Polynesians did invade the empty islands of the Pacific, not drift by chance upon them) began with the century.

A farmer with an eye to the main chance—which was, quite simply, getting out—lopped land from his farm and sold it in quarter-acre and half-acre slices. What prompted him was the rising number of excursionists, one-day trippers, from the city. They liked the peace and quiet, they said, and littered his land. In a manner of speaking, then, he had his revenge. He sold and they bought and built. Then he left.

The main occupation on Motutangi became lack of occupation.

On cheap land the holidaymakers built cheap cottages, occupied at least once and at most three or four times a year.

In the depression came the unemployed. They lived on the dole and home-grown vegetables. And fish, when sea and weather offered.

Thirdly, more or less with the consolidation of the welfare state on the mainland, came the retired. Some were the holidaymakers of an earlier time, now on pensions.

And there were always, of course, the unemployable.

In time the island came to possess a dozen settlements, six post offices, two banks, four churches. Also two pubs, three vineyards, four schools, one doctor and one policeman, and five thousand people.

They clustered tightly, as might be expected, on that portion of the island nearest the city. Almost as if ready to leap back again, should the island sink.

Geography: climate. The climate of Motutangi is, according to texts available, semi-tropical. Which means it never snows but it rains, and bananas sometimes ripen.

Still, statistics say the island is on average between five and ten degrees Fahrenheit warmer than neighbouring mainland. Temptation enough. Most winters are frostless. Since the elderly are vulnerable to cold, estate agents are eager to advise retirement to sunny Motutangi. They cannot offer properties in great variety, or quantity, but their turnover is immense. Sooner or later, over a period of five or ten years, most properties are back on the market again.

Economics. The island has no economy. It is a virtual appendage of the social security department. The one prospect it ever had of self-sufficiency, as a popular holiday resort, was liquidated by the internal combustion engine. City-dwellers began to find it easier to get to holiday places by road than by water. For a brief and tantalizing period wartime petrol-rationing seemed likely to turn traffic back to Motutangi. But postwar prosperity, and the welfare state, made the island's situation certain. Resorts north and south of the city flourished, Motutangi languished. Yet hopes still spring like weeds from asphalt. These days rumours persist that a Rockefeller is about to snap the entire place up as a retreat for world-weary millionaires. But the only Americans to appear so far have been those in a tiny and impoverished Californian group looking for an island refuge from nuclear war: they stayed a month, then went home to California.

Culture. The island has two moving-picture houses, also used as dance halls in summer, and an estimated eight hundred television sets.

Trade. Motutangi once produced milk, meat and vegetables not only for itself but for the city. Now milk, meat and vegetables arrive daily by boat from the city.

Architecture. The houses of Motutangi, almost with no exception, are wooden. They have a suburban density at the city end of the island, and thin out rapidly towards the other end. Many are the original shacks. Most are roughly square in shape, roofed with corrugated iron. They can have anything from one to five rooms, but seldom more. In a functional age, they function.

History again. What can Motutangi tell the twentieth century? Consider the society. Of birth, copulation and death, the first is insignificant, statistically; the second seldom detectable beyond the holiday season; the third never less than prominent. As elsewhere it is usually well heralded by illness or accident. It is observed, however, with unusually intense interest. Windows fly open the length of a street, sometimes the length of a settlement, when the island's antique ambulance comes calling. On the other hand there are people so far retired from the world that only flies, or faint smells, call attention to their departure. People sometimes vanish. Presumed to be visiting relatives on the mainland perhaps, they are found days or weeks later in the tide. It might have been a fall from a cliff-edge path, a slip on the rocks when casting a line, or a dinghy mishap. It might even have been something else, though the coroner seldom says so. Identification is sometimes difficult and next of kin impossible to locate.

On the whole there is a good deal of waiting on the island. The cemetery may not be the busiest place on Motutangi, as some wits like to have it, but aside from post offices on pension days it is as busy as most.

It would be unfair, though, to leave the impression that the island is only or entirely a refuge for the aged. However diminished its vague hopes, however tattered its precise expectations, it remains a resort of a kind. At least guest houses, private hotels, proliferate in optimism; and as often as not are burned down in despair. The island fire brigade is slow moving, its vehicle aged, and the insurance companies seldom find evidence. There are roughly two seasons: the holiday season, and the rest of the year. The holiday season begins at Christmas or just before, depending how weekends fall, and ends three weeks later. The rest of the year lasts forty-nine weeks. Of course a thin total of visitors, and temporary settlers, do make the trek across this quiet desert of time. And adulterers are as common as honeymooners. Still, sexual congress is by no means the only reason for refuge. During summer months elderly women painters, spinsters and widows mainly, prowl the more picturesque hills and beaches south of Te Hianinu Bay, the furthest settled reach of the island, and said to attract a better class of people in retirement; at least some obscure statistics are produced to prove the professions are better represented there. Just back of Te Hianinu Bay, moreover, there is a nudist colony in a ferny valley. Though the island has few cultural conceits Te Hianinu Bay did have at one time a Scottish castle, which collapsed for want of good foundations, and a house decorated like an Eastern temple smelling of incense within. From time to time there are rumours of homosexual groups, organized by otherwise respected citizens, contriving improbable orgies in and around Te Hianinu Bay. And, whatever its pretensions, it is true that the bay, as against the rest of the island, does attract the occasional writer or artist. These, though, are rare and inconspicuous. They work quietly and anonymously and then slip away again, often rather too swiftly; they are not identified until it is too late for the residents of Te Hianinu Bay to claim them as the bay's own. But this, after all, is but one disappointment among many.

A sanctuary for life's walking wounded? No one lives long on Motutangi without more than sufficient reason.

But man, man the social animal, creature of custom?

Last year a man advertised in the local paper for a rifle, in good condition, to settle a dispute with a neighbour. This neighbour retaliated by dynamiting his adversary's outdoor lavatory.

Another pair of neighbours, both in their seventies, fenced fiercely with hedge-clippers; and damaged each other almost beyond reasonable repair. Until that day they had been on excellent terms. One had accused the other of obscenely ogling his young wife. His wife is sixty.

Mrs Daisy Banks, widow, of Moewai settlement, complained to the police about the flying saucers which landed regularly on the roof of her two-roomed cottage. Their crews, she explained, monitored her conversations. Mrs Banks lives alone and never has visitors.

A retired sea captain asserted that he had been persistently and maliciously cheated by a certain storekeeper. On his veranda he set up a small old cannon, which he had evidently restored to working order, pointed directly at the store. When the police arrived at his front gate he managed with effort to swivel it in their direction, but then blew himself up.

One of the island's few remaining farmers objected to another farmer making use of a certain private road. They fought a duel with bulldozers. As fast as the first farmer ploughed up his own road, out of spite, the second filled it in again. Their noise was enough to alert half the island, and there were some two hundred spectators before they finally crashed head-on and separated to fetch shotguns. Then the police arrived.

A poison-pen correspondent responsible for a half-dozen devastated marriages and at least two suicides was at last revealed (after four years) as sweet little old Miss Hester Hutchins, spinster and good churchwoman of Te Hianinu Bay. Miss Hutchins had long had the pleasant reputation of always having a special smile for everyone.

A retired trade-union leader claimed that Communists were trying to poison him. Further, he claimed that his grocer and butcher were

Communist agents. He began fetching his food personally from the mainland, but claimed always to be followed on these excursions. He fell from the ferry one evening, apparently in flight from something, and his body was later dragged from the sea.

A proposal to destroy all trees along the Te Hianinu foreshore roused even more feverish passions than usual in a place never noted for cool controversy. Nature-lovers asserted that the trees enhanced life. Sex-haters argued that the dense trees offered concealment and positive incitement to indecent activity, particularly in holiday season. The issue is still lively, but it has been observed that the two sides are saying more or less the same thing.

A wedding on the island is an uncommon event, and this community celebrated three last year. In the course of the most interesting of these the bride struck the groom with a hammer, and the bride's mother broke three of his ribs. After attention from a doctor, the groom was returned to the wedding breakfast—and his shy bride—in plaster.

A vigilante group was formed to help control gangs of violent louts and noisy long-hairs who make sporadic appearances on the island through the holiday season. To general regret the inaugural meeting of this group, called in a homebrewer's shed, ended in confusion and finally in one of the islands most notable brawls in recent years.

Mrs Sarah Blue, proprietress of the Heavenly Haven guest house, objected to her delinquent husband's prolonged stays in the bar of the Motutangi Bowling Club. At the height of the bowling season, during a grand tournament, she undressed entirely, by way of protest, on number one green. The game continued.

The holiday season excepted (it is always an exception, which proves no rule) the island is boasted as virtually crime free. True, there was a murder some years ago, and a few attempted murders since; and last summer a teenage boy shot his twin sister. The verdict, however, was death by misadventure.

And this summer?

TWO

For the winter does end. And the rain, which lasts through the holiday season and afterwards subsides.

By the time the sun comes they are quite comfortable. Homely, Ted likes to say. There are curtains on the windows, rugs on the floor. Amazing, Ted says, what she's been able to do with the old shack.

'But, after all,' he always adds, 'we're not going to be here long. I mean, what's the point?'

'The point is that this is the only home we have,' Jean replies. 'I might as well make it pleasant.'

'Have it your own way,' he sighs. 'It's not as if this is the only place we'll have.'

'I wish I could be sure about that,' she says. She likes to be frank on this subject.

'How long do you think we can stay on this damn island anyway?' he asks.

'That's up to you, surely.'

'Don't get scratchy again.'

'I'm not scratchy.'

'You are. I can tell.' He is amused. 'You can't keep anything a secret.'

'Because I've got no secrets. I like to be honest. Which is more than I can say for–' She bites off the end of the sentence, for all the good that does; her agitation is even more apparent.

'For who?' he smiles. He reclines lazily in an old wicker chair. His eyes are half closed, with the provocative pretence of weariness, as he watches her move about the room. 'For me?'

She doesn't say anything. She goes on with what she is doing. She is mounting a print to hang on the wall.

'Come on,' he says. 'Out with it. Let's get it over.'

'Then what was that letter you got yesterday?'

'You know. You know perfectly well.'

This is true. She does know. 'Then what did she say? You haven't told me.'

'The usual. You know it all.'

'I don't know that I do.'

'All is forgiven, Teddy darling. Come home again. You know.'

'I see.'

'Read it if you like.'

'No thank you.' Jean has never met Ted's wife. And the less she knows, the better. She wants nothing of his past; she needs a pristine present. She sees a letter as possible contamination.

'Scared?' he suggests, with some accuracy.

'Just not interested.'

He laughs. 'Come here,' he says. 'Relax.'

She is fumbling with the print now. Her hands have grown clumsy. 'Come on,' he coaxes.

But her voice remains steady, if not her hands. 'And the children?' she asks. 'Did she mention them?'

'Here and there. Amid all the breast-beating.'

'What about the divorce?'

'She has nothing to say about that. Regrettably enough.'

'I see.'

'It'll be all right, though.'

'How? How can it be all right?'

'It will be,' he predicts with confidence. Oddly, his confidence was what she once liked most about him.

'And what am I supposed to do in the meantime?' She feels her voice might crack with the sudden pressure behind it.

'Aren't you forgetting something?' he says casually.

'What?'

'Me. We're in this together.'

'You're not committed. Not like I am.'

'No?'

'No. You can fall back on your wife, your family. What have I got to fall back on? Nothing.'

'Then I would have thought I was risking everything,' he observes. 'In that case. You have an odd way of looking at things.'

'I can't help it. That's the way it is.'

'Come here,' he says. 'Come on.'

'I'm going out,' she protests weakly. 'Just as soon as I finish this.'

'Come on.'

Finally she goes to him. But still clumsy, tall and clumsy. She sits at his feet and he places an arm about her shoulder. With his free hand he strokes her loose hair.

'I was going out,' she explains, 'to give you a chance to be alone. You haven't had much chance since we've been here The weather and everything.'

For the moment he has nothing to say. His hand drops from her hair to her neck. She shivers.

'All right?' he asks.

'Yes, Ted. All right.'

'And what do you want me to be alone for?'

'I feel you need to be. That's all. You've got to have a chance to think things out.'

'What things?'

'Your future, for one thing.'

'Who wants to think?' he says.

'You do. You ought to.'

'Enough's enough. I've done my thinking.'

'What do you mean?'

She looks at him, uncertain, and he kisses her. 'Not to worry,' he says lightly. And she trembles.

He is stooping now, gathering her up. Or at least trying to. A shabby couch appears to be his destination.

'No,' she says, bracing herself 'No, Ted.'

'What's wrong?'

For they have arrived at the couch. A broken spring claws her back. She attempts to roll out from under him. 'It's not an answer,' she says feebly. 'It's not an answer to everything. It can't be.'

THREE

She is outside again.

It is the third day he has seen the girl. He has never been followed before. Or is the word haunted? If the latter, never has there been a more melancholy apparition. Her clothes might have been those hastily offered some naked, shivering survivor of accident; and they never change, not even in the heat of noon. Perhaps they are as permanent as her ghostly complexion. An enormously oversize red jumper, unravelling wildly at the elbows, commands the eye. Then jeans torn at one knee, patched at the other. A huge chain of wooden beads, which clacks faintly when she moves, hangs in swinging coils about her neck. She wears an entirely shapeless hat; it may originally have been a man's. And she is barefoot. Barefoot on the dusty clay road, outside his cottage. A slender book rests on her upturned palms. She reads it intently, never seeming to turn a page. He fancies her lips move now and then, but he is not near enough to be sure. She seems the image of a pilgrim. Or . . .

But he cannot locate a direction for the thought. He lets fall the curtain of his front window, and retreats creakily into the modestly solid protection of his walls.

The worst thing, the really wretched thing, is that she seems familiar. Not so much in her appearance as in her face. There is something gently vacant about her face. Attractive? He supposes not. It is a dour face, dull of feature, pale to an extreme, and lightly freckled. He doubts if it could improve with closer observation. And it is not a face especially to remember, though apparently he does, or may. But from where? It is that gentle vacancy which troubles him. That is familiar. He has seen that vacancy, or something like it, on rank after rank of fresh young faces upturned.

If that is all, then the familiarity is all surface, easily explained. He cannot conceive that she has ever belonged among those other faces, ever been one of his students. Even the idea she might is laughable, in its way.

But he does not laugh.

He sits uneasily to his self-made breakfast. A boiled egg and toast is usually sufficient to see him through the long days. And this day promises to be longer than most. He has risen early, after a restless night, to find the girl materialized outside his cottage again.

Imagination, then? Even in his most fanciful flight, she would have been improbable. And she is, besides, all too palpable. He resists the impulse to return to the window; he feels a faint prickle of fright.

They have not spoken. There have been no words at all. He chips the top off his egg and then pushes it aside uneaten. The idea of eating it has become as distasteful as the thought that he may eventually have to speak to her. Possibly it is all mistaken identity. She mistakes him for someone else, or something else. That may well be. Some old deceitful lover? That is a joke too.

He still does not laugh, though. Or even feel like laughing. He tastes the toast, which is cold.

Other people on the island, in Te Hianinu Bay, will soon notice, almost certainly, and begin to talk; and may have already. For all he knows, and he never knows much about other people in the bay.

Six months' peace, quite gone. The coffee has grown cold too.

He decides he should have spoken to the girl, perhaps passed comment on the weather, the first time he noticed her near. Speech would have been easier then; it is difficult now. The prospect is as much embarrassing as distasteful.

Another point is that a girl—or woman?—of her appearance can scarcely go unremarked, even on Motutangi, even at this time of year.

The Professor a subject of scandal? Who better? Since his arrival on the island he has kept all human contact to a minimum, and that is nothing new anyway; he has found, with the years, most casual contact avoidable.

Suppose she is an idiot, merely? That pale, dull face at least conveys the impression. And the thought offers him a moment's relief. Though that is all.

It is hard to recall exactly when he became aware of her, that first day. Aware in the sense that she became something significantly more than a lone figure in seascape. She rather seemed to have sprouted, without preliminary, from the beach itself. For a time she occupied only a corner of his vision; perhaps his eyes passed over that wild costume, and passed on. He continued, anyway, with his usual walk: the time of day does not dictate this walk, rather the time of tide. Which to him means simply that he has learned, after a half dozen months, to live with tide rather than time; within rhythm rather than vacuum. A rhythm which accommodates gracefully. At least he finds it so. And Te Hianinu's mile-long beach is ideal for a brisk walk at low tide. After the length of the beach there are the headlands where, with the tide at ebb, black reefs and shiny rock-pools rise. This disputed region, daily contested by sea and land (or air, or moon?) has become his own; here his own dissonances dwindle and drown in cosmic flux. After all, a mirror so huge and exact can only diminish. He moves with caution from rock to slippery rock, his heart often clamouring as he stoops to explore crevices. It is not really the fascination with such places he remembers as a child, for then his interest was in the pools, with tiny living things: anenomes, shrimps, crabs. Now he fossicks among sea's dead tribute to shore, seawrack and driftwood, as though in search of messages. And sometimes he finds, or appears to find, what he seeks: among other things he collects starfish, emblems of worlds unknown. Sometimes still with a cringe of life, cast up by storm, and sometimes dead; and sometimes, when he wades with protected feet among the oyster beds, caught gliding over sand or stuck fast to rock.

It is an interest. Or so he believes; he tells himself he is at the time of life when one must find new interests or perish. And he has already almost perished. At the graveside of his wife, less than a year ago, if one time among several is to be named: he listened to the minister's melancholy words falling, watched loose soil and tiny lumps of clay dribble down upon the lowered coffin. He had listened to such words, or something very like them, often enough before; he had, after all, attended church with his wife most Sundays of his married life. And it wasn't, at his age, his first funeral. He had always, in fact, found such words pleasant and comforting enough, at least in tone; his mind was usually elsewhere. Not far away, true, but with the living rather than the dead, or with memory of the dead. Faith had been a screen upon which his thoughts could at random play; at other times a thread, glimmering here, glimmering there, in the fabric of existence, so much of which anyway could be taken for granted. Until now: until this moment when he watched soil and clay dribble quietly, almost furtively, over the grave's brink; noted that it had been heaped untidily, too close to the edge; and listened. With his mind opened wholly, perhaps for the first time. The words entered and collapsed without sound, without echo; they might never have been. The earth dribbled finely, then ceased. And that was all. He might later have moved among the thin collection of mourners, shaking hands, offering thanks—his wife and he had never many friends, few of them shared—and in fact he has the impression he may have done so, though he cannot recall it. On the other hand he also has the impression that he was guided tearless from the graveside, made comfortable in some vehicle. Not that these impressions are in essence contradictory, or even matter a great deal: the point is just that no further details had significance. He was already adrift.

Of course it took time to acknowledge. There was his work, for one thing; the receding ranks of fresh faces beneath the high ceiling of the lecture-theatre. For one thing? For everything. That was something else he came to learn. His marriage was childless, and though once he might have wished it different the fact had never been a thing for grief: there had always been his work. As there was now; he might never have had the time, the attention and above all the patience for children anyway. There was no conceivable place for them in his life. Which, to tell the truth, was always comfortable. If his life knew no great effort, nor great passion, it was at least coloured by devotion. His love for his work was real enough. His love for his wife too, even if a more cautious thing. Sometimes it seemed he never recovered from his surprise when she, so young then, accepted him. At all events he never got to know her well, as he acknowledged to himself with some pain during the illness which preceded her death. They were always a quiet couple, as quiet when young as in old age. And old age, until her illness and death, was a painless affair. His life was never unhappy. And hers? Perhaps she felt the barren condition of their marriage more keenly than he, but there was no way of knowing; they never spoke of it.

If there were someone with whom he might have conversed after the funeral, everything might have been different. But there was only ever one person in whom he confided, and then only partially, and now Margaret was dead. And on reflection he saw he might also have been denied her understanding. Her evident pleasure in his work, his scholarship, might just have been wifely pretence. He became haunted by a malicious self-portrait of himself when young, at the time Margaret met him — a sober and humourless pedant, prematurely middle-aged. Could she ever have expected much? He must have promised neither passion nor the mildest excitement, a marginal life at best. For now the comfort of their past grew like an accusation; their past, his life. What had he done with it, and what was the point? That was what it amounted to. His life, not hers. Absurd to pretend that she ever had one of her own. She gave it to his, but for what?

He might have had some answer at the graveside, when he needed it, but he had nothing. His life was always lived on the assumption that there was a general scheme of things, into which he fitted inconspicuously, like Margaret in his own life, but when it came to the point—he had quite evidently spent all of a life, bulky with qualifying footnotes, coming to the point—he was blind, utterly blind, to such a general scheme. Which was not to deny its possibility, if ever he could get a foothold again. But where? His was a life without extremes. Others might find revelation in the marvellous and the violent. He was as much a stranger to the marvellous as to the violent; and his country seemed hardly the place for revelation anyway. It had been woken from the longest sleep in history to flinch beneath the whip and knife of human enterprise, and was now gently subsiding into sleep again. Taking its human occupants, who had clearly done as much as they wanted, along on the drowsy journey too. On a map of the world in his study, towards which he began to incline his gaze in fretful moments, the country hung suspended in emptiness between the Asian and American continents, between present and past, present and future, like a tilted hammock perhaps; and offering a void into which unnumbered lives might slip without trace. And without reason. Lives such as his own, for example, or Margaret's.

It was a country where the obvious became more so.

Dark began congealing in corners of his mind; he encountered it with a shock and dismay which never lessened, perhaps increased. Even work offered no cleansing. Yet for two or three months he read, wrote and lectured as if there were no change in his circumstances at all. Until the possible impermanence or irrelevance of the word began to oppress him quite as much as the impermanence of the flesh. He had of course never been a winner of truths, a maker of knowledge, but rather a vehicle; a means of conveyance for wiser men. Every prophet must have his scribes, and though he had never aspired to the condition of prophet, nor resented his role as scribe, he began now to doubt his adequacy as much as his accuracy. If truth were meant to move and change, what happened to it in his recitation? Was it his work then, and the work of those like him, to defuse truth, make it harmless? So that yesterday's wisdom became tomorrow's platitude? And the world went on as before, unchanged and unrevealed.

But that was just one thing among many.

The lecture theatre was filled that afternoon. The ranks of bent heads, the open notebooks, the scratching pens. He stopped, quite abruptly, in mid-sentence. It seemed to him that all light, all meaning, in the words he spoke was extinguished in the very instant he uttered them. The pens were paused, the heads still bent. He began again. And once more he had the sensation of words going out without meaning, without echo, collapsing much as they had upon his ears on the day of Margaret's funeral. Now there was a faint stir of impatience in the lecture theatre; heads were lifted, pens set down. It seemed he had faltered again, or stopped altogether, and was looking at them in silent appeal. There was curiosity on some faces, and—was it?—frank boredom on others. At this stage, with the minute-hand of the clock close to the full hour, he should have been summing up the theme of the lecture, drawing it gracefully to a close; he always prided himself on precision in these matters. He disliked untidiness, ideas carelessly unravelled and left at that; it was irresponsible, and contemptuous besides. The silence grew oppressive; the sun played through the large windows of the theatre, dust motes turned in its rays, and he heard his own breathing. Quite distinctly, almost as final evidence.

'The point,' he said, and listened; there was a flutter as the heads bent again and pages were turned. 'The point is that there isn't.'

He groped, he began, he took flight. Presently faces flicked up into his sight, signalling perplexity and alarm. Words jumbled from his mouth thick and heavy, fell crashing, toppled trees in a rain of leaves. As if all that encircled and oppressed were now receding, leaving him conspicuous and alone, but inwardly at peace. The minute-hand closed with the hour and travelled beyond. Still the words rushed, fell.

But something stuck, finally.

'You see,' he began to repeat. 'You see.'

And his hands began to reach into the air wildly; he might have been trying to move something immense, but quite invisible to those around.

At length, anyway, it was clear what had happened. Three or four of the more mature students approached him, circled diffidently, and then took his arms to lead him away. It was then he began to weep— for them, or for himself, or from frustration, he could never be sure.

His professional colleagues were sympathetic, much as they had been about Margaret. They wished him, they said, a quick recovery. He was able, quite coolly, to imagine their headshaking behind his back, and their reopened wounds of ambition; the chances were his long-held chair would fall vacant. He was happy, in the end, to give them this satisfaction. He resigned, and retired. He was not even interested in his successor. Te Hianinu Bay, on Motutangi, was far enough away. Irrelevant things soon became remote.

Already he has doubtless passed into student legend. 'Professor Thomson?' he can imagine them saying. 'Wasn't he the one who went off his head in a lecture? Started talking gibberish? You mean you were actually there, that day?'

A story like that might prove rather durable, worth embellishing.

So he has started again. In a bay, on an island. But is he really far enough away?

That girl. Who is she? He ransacks his past, and once more returns empty-handed. And anyway if she does belong there, if she does really know him, she should surely have spoken by now.

That day, that first day, he was moving carefully about a headland haunt when he observed her standing near. She had a book beneath her arm—a book was almost part of her costume—and regarded him with an entirely impassive face. There was no mistake. Her interest was in him, in what he was doing.

At once he felt foolish. There was no ignoring her. As if she could be ignored anyway.

He tried to take an interest in his search again, but this outlandish bystander made it impossible. Her gaze unnerved him. Not that he acknowledged her presence in any way. He didn't even make a friendly nod in her direction. Residence on Motutangi has taught him care in these things. The slightest friendly gesture can lead to a garrulous avalanche, feverish offers of intimacy.

At times he even thinks Motutangi is not for such as himself. He would shift, perhaps, if he knew where. And if he stays, it is not entirely for lack of somewhere better, but also because sea and sky, hill and headland, the peace of an island, have made a claim. To be fair, it possibly also makes claim on those others, also retired from the world, whom he avoids. Possibly, though there is not much sign of it. They seem to live among themselves and upon themselves, seldom looking outward. The sea holds fish for the table, and the sky rain for the garden, sun for the ripening of fruit, and this, after all, is reasonable. At least they are still in touch with the business of the world. He could offer the island a garden himself, instead of harvesting the dead things of the shore.

Curiosity, then? But her interest in him did not cease when he left the rocks. She followed him home, at a distance. It was the same the day after; and the same yesterday. And today she is outside the cottage, waiting.

Perhaps, if he continues to ignore her, she will go away, disappear back to wherever she belongs. Though where can that be? Already, for him, she has become part of the island, part of his day. He cannot envisage her elsewhere, and that is the trouble.

He rises from the breakfast table and returns to the window. She has not gone away. She is still very much there. If she has changed her position in the least, even turned a page of her book, it is not apparent.

Low tide. Time for his walk. That is, if he plans it today.

FOUR

The boy goes slowly out into the morning.

It is a fine morning, brisk with breeze, and Hau hill stands up sharply in the sunlight. Yet a morning not so unlike any other lately, though warmer.

Ahead is time. That is all. If his gaze upon the morning is bleak, so is his view of time.

Behind, his parents hover. He has only one clear aim, this morning and most mornings, and that is to escape their sight.

He walks slowly, methodically, past tree and around ridge until he no longer feels their gaze. Then he stops and has the morning to himself, for what it is worth. He slumps to the grass, between random boulders, in an eroded gully on the side of Hau hill. It is a place where he is unlikely to be discovered or disturbed. Around are young pines, with a strong summery smell of resin, and directly below, at the foot of a perilously steep incline, is the sea. Giant pohutukawa grow down there, limbs laced, leaves bright, roots gripping hill and rock against the attack of the sea. He also has a view of the entire length of Te Hianinu Bay, though he evidently does not think this worth examination.

After a time he rolls over and buries his face in the grass. His feet begin to kick down at the hard earth. At first lightly, almost tentatively; then bruisingly.

Time. He has it all to himself, really.

His parents turn from the window eventually, and retreat into themselves again. For a time they do not speak. Their silence is thick with a familiar despair. So someone has to talk finally, if only for the sound of the words, the comfort of speech. For the words are familiar too.

FIVE

ple

c/o Te Hianinu P.O.
Motutangi

Dear Chris [*he writes*], Forgive the intrusion but I perhaps optimistically imagine you're wondering where I am. The above address should be sufficient answer. Yes, I know it may have been unkind of me to leave without warning, but you gave me little option. Rather your behaviour left me little option, if you can see what I mean. Perhaps you can't. So let me make it clear that my departure, however abrupt, was really for your own good. And no hard feelings. At least there are none on my side.

How did I come to get here? Well, it's simple. You remember that funny plump fellow Chappy Gordon we always seemed to be striking at Freddy's place? He often mentioned to me that he had a most secluded little hideaway on this island, if ever I wanted one. No motive; I think the fellow was being genuinely friendly. And he wasn't at all surprised when I took him up on it at last. He said I was welcome and could have it as long as I liked, since he rarely has use for it himself now. He gave me the key without any conditions—no, Chris, none at all—when I looked him up in his city office (he's a lawyer, of all things). We went out to lunch together and then I left the city at top speed.

In case you suspect otherwise, by the way, I live here quite alone. Quite, quite alone. I won't say that I never see anyone from one day to the next, because it wouldn't be true. One must mix with the natives on occasion; I mean I have to pick up meat and groceries.

Te Hianinu Bay has the reputation of being the most exclusive and

33

.sant part of the island. I wouldn't know. All I can say is, God help .ne rest. Imagine a collection of huts or boxes, squalid little confections of decaying wood, sometimes painted, more often peeling, scattered along and above and around a perfect dream of a white Pacific beach. There you have it, more or less. True, there's much pleasant open countryside around, farmed in a desultory way, and a quite exquisite coastline, virtually virginal, on each side. Still it scarcely compensates for the stark horror of the actual bay, and all those boxy little lives in a sylvan slum. You have to see it to believe it.

The locals? Since I've been here only two weeks I'm still feeling my way (make what you like of that). One thing is, for a village this place has a city-size collection of village idiots. True. Mongoloids, all kinds. I thought at first—seeing so many—there must be some kind of institution in the vicinity. Not at all. They're just normally resident. The kind of people one evidently finds flung out towards the periphery of cities, into the discard. The people who just can't make it. This place is more than just a refuge for the retired. It's a haven for the mentally crippled as well as the physically maimed and decayed. There's something quite sick, rather chilling about it all. Or is that just because I am identifying with them? Please don't smile. As for the rest, there are the retired—in various states of physical decay, one faculty or another going or gone, and in various stages of senility. Oh yes, and the shopkeepers. God knows how they survive. One holiday season to the next, I suppose. Their faces are usually as grim as their prices. Transport costs from the city, they explain, when overdressed old ladies mutter around the shop. But the old ladies continue to mutter. Do I paint too black a picture? Conceded my nose for the normal isn't what it used to be, but I'm sure there is ordinary life here too. I mean I know for a fact that some people live here with their families and commute to work in the city. All I can plead is that they're not much in evidence, even at weekends. Their children are, of course. There are schools on the island, though I hate to imagine the average I.Q. What I mean is, I do see children now and then; there is evidence that the human race has a future, though I wouldn't know how much or what kind.

And what do I do here? I watch, I listen, I play the voyeur. But that's a very tame role on this island. A way of passing the time. Like the walking and swimming I engage in. I contrive mysteries which probably have some fantastically simple solution; that is, I observe, collect and frame them for hanging in the corridors of my mind. Thus I spend much time in splendid meditation, not entirely navel-regarding. I recognize, of course, that this interest—this absorption in the affairs of others—is just another way of avoiding myself, like the act of living on this island.

This negates, rather, what I'm about to say or explain to you, but I shall say it nevertheless. I'm not coming back. Don't ask me what I'm going to do. I don't look ahead further than this summer. I mean I'm here for the summer and, with any luck, the rest of my life will look after itself. But why am I really here? I think perhaps to find if I can be alone. I don't mean *live* alone—almost any fool can rise to the occasion there. I mean be alone, and yet content within myself. No, that's not it either. That's giving the thing the glamour I hope precisely to avoid. Perhaps the word 'alone' isn't adequate, yet I must make do. I just want to get used to being alone, because I know I must. Ignore the paradox and take that on trust. And, all right, smile. Smile you bastard smile.

He draws a line through the last sentence and, upon further reflection, carefully inks it out.

I know you will think this unrealistic. Never mind. You probably imagine you know enough about me, in fact, to be certain that this is fantasy on my part, a dream from which I'll awaken in a short time. Perhaps. We'll see. When I look back on my life, I am perfectly aware that it amounts to little. I should dread to list the things I have attempted, the lives I've tried to live. Sometimes I have even proved proficient; but never good, and never lasting. Now I'm still a dilettante, a playboy with one foot (perhaps both, now) in middle age. In place of my earlier ambitions—rather sweet in retrospect—I had simply the creation of my own personality. More or less. The fact is I now find that personality distasteful—what I own of it, that is. For a personality is a collective possession. Other people own it, perhaps more than oneself. No, come to think, other people own it altogether. I own nothing. Nothing. Nothing. What I've come here to do is to see if I really have anything, something at all slightly resembling myself, worth salvage. I can only do that alone. I mean if I can't do it alone, I can't do it at all.

Please don't take this letter as an invitation to come and see me. I don't want that at all. I'm writing simply because I owe you an explanation—and, well, because you're about the only person to whom I can write, to whom anything I say might make some kind of sense. Though I know it won't. I'm sure it won't. You've got a mean, cruel mind, always seeking the worst. I know that because I know the same qualities in myself; perhaps you brought them to the surface.

He begins deleting again.

Later [*he writes*] . . . I've just been for a longish walk, quite a relief. A warm pleasant morning, a breeze, the tide low, the long beach almost bare. Not much in the way of humanity for this voyeur to observe, yet quite enough. I've collected myself another little mystery as well as noting my pet one. Perhaps I ought to tell you about the latter first. It concerns an elderly gentleman I've seen often over the past couple of weeks. Apparently resident here. I've taken him for some kind of nut, and I still hold that opinion in reserve. For some reason I see him only at low tide, as if he's something the sea regularly leaves behind. He has a rather lean pinched face, yellowy and distinctly unhealthy, with thick spectacles heavy on his bony nose. His body, what one can observe of it, is merely something upon which clothes can be hung. Always rather formally dressed, which marks him out here. He potters along the beach, his lips moving, his eyes sightless, seeming to be in endless conversation with himself. Then he snuffles round the rocks at the end of the beach as if he's looking for something he lost a long time ago. Never talks to anyone, at least no one I've seen. That is what makes my more recent observation intriguing. (He might have just paled into the background for me had I not learned, by way of eavesdropping on grocery-store gossip, that he is or was a university professor who arrived here last year.) The fact is, he's being followed. No, not by the police, unless they assume the most unlikely of disguises these days. By a girl, a perfect fright of a creature. I put her down as another of the island's nuts, the moment I saw her, and I've no reason to qualify the opinion. This has been going on for three or four days now. I assume even he must have been aware of it before today; anyway he was certainly aware of her this morning. At first she just plodded along the shore behind him, at a fairly discreet distance, but every now and then increasing her pace as if she were about to approach him and speak. But she never did, or does. Though she has, while I've watched, been gaining confidence. Where before she only followed him part way along the beach, now she follows him full length. Without any pretence of not following, as if he and she were the only two people in the world. Fascinating. Otherwise there is no indication that they know each other. She might be following him at random, and perhaps she is. In that case I hope she doesn't start following me instead. On the other hand perhaps he has been aware of her from the beginning, and is only now beginning to feel really uncomfortable, as I certainly would. This is logical and reasonable. And offers me a clue. She is clearly his illegitimate daughter, the byproduct of some most regrettably lusty episode in the years of his declining virility, come back to claim him as father. No? It has a Victorian flavour, and such revelations are saved for the third act. All right, so she's his daughter—allow me that guess—but one he dumped in an institution, for idiocy rather than illegitimacy, years ago. Now she is forcing him to acknowledge her—in all her sickly splendour. That's not entirely satisfactory either. The thing that sticks is that she appears to be literate, and is certainly reading when not stalking him silently; I haven't seen her without a book. All right, one more guess. She is not his daughter but someone else's—I daren't think whose— but one he has briefly taken advantage of in a shameful and unscholarly way, in some dim recess of the university perhaps, and now cannot shake off. She is guilt incarnate and God knows she looks the part. She will haunt him until he either reciprocates her love, in his fashion, or drowns himself for his folly. The scene certainly suits. I wish I could convey the flavour of the thing, the long beach, the sea and sky, and these two tiny figures. Perfect for a crime of passion. Actually it's hard to think of anything more unlikely, with that pair. I must guess again or wait and see. This morning he was decidedly aware of her anyway. He kept looking over his shoulder and cut short his usual visit to the rocks at each end of the beach. He no sooner arrived at one end than he set off home again, the girl an increasing distance behind. She looked dejected. I'm sure they didn't speak. She didn't follow him off the beach. Instead she collapsed in the shade of one of the trees fringing the beach (incidentally it might delight you to know that these trees are under threat of destruction, being so invitingly sexy). And read her book. She is always hopelessly overdressed. From a distance she appeared to be just a shapeless heap of clothes dumped in the sand. Then one could observe with surprise the grubby face peering out.

The new mystery is by contrast rather ordinary, though it affects me more. After I'd witnessed the morning performance of the professor and his (?), I took myself along his usual route to the south end of the beach, where dwellings become sparse and finally fade out altogether. There is rarely anyone about there, apart from the odd shellfish-gatherer, and no one this morning but a single woman bather. Now that had its moment of mystery too, come to think. As I recall it, she looked at me, and I looked right back at her. Without a word, but as if we knew each other. Certainly there seemed to be recognition of some kind. Perhaps we do know each other. Perhaps we've met at someone's party. A common enough thing. I wonder how many people one meets and forgets in an average year. Especially with my kind of life; what depresses me is it seems my kind of death. Anyway I passed this near-naked hussy by, whoever she is, and continued to the end of the beach. The once I looked back, she'd gone her way too, well out into the calm bay, a very strong swimmer. A cooler choice for exercise than mine. Looming at the south end of the beach is a large hill. Hau hill is the local name, quite a landmark, once a Maori fortress (you can see the bumps left by trenches around the blunt summit), with a long lumpy headland clinging like a tail to its shaggy head. Excellent for exercise. I climbed up a steep flank with effort but no great difficulty, and when I paused for breath near the summit I grew aware of an odd sound. At first I thought an opossum (they make eerie sounds in the bush about Chappy's hideaway at night, sometimes quite disturbing) but then I realized it was human. A human grieving, with a tinge of hysteria. More unnerving than an opossum in that lonely place. I moved quietly around the summit towards the sound—guiltily too, I should add, for I was clearly intruding. Or is the guilt we feel on these occasions because we don't feel or share the grief, but feel we ought, for common humanity's sake? I stalked the sound down to some boulders off to the side of the hill, cluttering a narrow gully. Unforgivably an intruder now, I moved round the boulders, keeping to the cover of some young pines, able to observe yet not be seen. What I saw was disappointing. At first.

What had I expected, perhaps hoped for? Some tragic love scene? In a sense I suppose it could have been, or the fag-end of one at least. For there was only one participant—and me, the audience. I had nothing but what I saw. And that was a lean long-limbed boy, brown with sun and naked apart from a pair of swimshorts, tumbled face down on some patchy grass. No, it wasn't an apparition, or a wishful illusion on my part. He was real, I insist. Real yet at the same time fantastic. With those pale boulders and dark pines about, he—or his figure—might have belonged to some romantic illustration. Please don't sneer. He was as real as uncanny. He could have been as young as fifteen, or as old as eighteen. And, yes, he was weeping—or grieving, rather. For the tears, if there had been any, were long dry. Thus he seemed rather animal in his pain. He writhed with it, his face distorted; again more purely animal than human. At first, naturally, I thought he might have hurt himself in some fall—might have just collapsed there in physical agony. I all but went to help him when I felt an inner signal, a warning flash, that his pain was private. I was sure he would prickle and escape in alarm, a wild creature, if I approached him and spoke. So I didn't, I didn't do anything. Except listen to those dry sobs subside. And as they did, I moved away. I climbed back toward the summit of Hau hill, my original destination, and by the time I made it everything around was quiet. There was just sound of surf on rocks far below. And a light, pleasantly fresh breeze. I stripped off and gave myself to the sun. Naturally I thought about the boy, the violence of whatever he felt, and probed memories of my own adolescence tenderly, in wonder. No real answer there, of course, though the violence had echo enough. I dozed and dreamed strangely —rather frighteningly, in fact—and then woke to my favourite (as of two weeks) view of the Pacific. Shadowy islands and remote blue ranges to my right; an unimpeded vista of ocean, unruffled and empty and soaring away to the tropics, to my left. And everywhere gulls, like bursts of blossom. I had it all to myself. As always, I felt regret on leaving the summit—partly the absurd sense of leaving questions unanswered, and unasked, up there. Absurd because if we had the words to ask, we would have the answers. What we haven't got, or have lost, is the language to converse with anything but ourselves, and even that not very well. We can no longer join dialogue with the non-human. And if we can't, how can we know ourselves at all?

Bear with me, please, if this letter's getting out of hand. I haven't spoken to anyone in two weeks. Unless one counts my purely functional conversation with grocer or publican.

I got down to the shore again and walked, rather bemused by my morning, along the sand. So preoccupied, in fact, that I bruised my shin nastily on a lump of driftwood. Then an unexpectedly high wave filled my shoes with water. (To tell the truth, this beach is usually a dead loss for surf, but it must have risen with the tide.) Thus I was in a fairly bloody mood—until there, dead in front of me, so close I could almost touch him, flashed away—down to the water—that boy. Yes, the same one. He looked completely recovered, as calm as they come. I was quite stunned. I watched him wade swiftly into the water and then dive beneath a wave. He rose vigorously on the other side and then swam out into the bay. A powerful swimmer and so he should be, with that long body. All the same, it was difficult to relate what I saw then—the impressive reserve and command of his face and figure as he strode into the sea as if he owned it—with what I had seen an hour or two before. Could emotion so violent really be ephemeral? Apparently. Anyway there he was, out in the sea. Now it seemed I was far more disturbed than he (perhaps having lost my romantic illustration) and, more bemused than ever, and rather dismayed, I wondered at his energy in the water. There might have been a fierce joy or exultation in his activity out there—something which could relate—but I couldn't trust my own observation. I had a double image I couldn't hope to focus. One thing I noticed was that he stayed well apart from the other swimmers on the beach (it was near noon, and they had increased in number).

I couldn't stare at him for ever. I began to feel conspicuous, for no good reason (there were few people near). So I walked further along the beach, towards home, and then ran into some unusual excitement. It seemed a shark had just been spotted off the beach. Hands pointed and there, sure enough, fifty to a hundred yards out, was a cruising fin. It was on an unchanging straight course, parallel with the beach, yet hesitating now and then as if seeking some way inshore. There were panicky people running and swimmers being called in all along the beach. Someone in the crowd claimed to have seen the same fin the day before. 'And I heard this was a *safe* beach,' said a woman in dismay, after pulling her children from the water. A shopkeeper who had rushed down to join the crowd looked glum. With a rainy holiday season and takings well down this year, a shark or two would be just enough to finish him, and a few like him, around here. Meantime, swimmers were rising from the water everywhere and walking unnerved and dripping up the sand, looking back now and then at that lonely fin. All very dramatic. At length everyone was warned and clear of the water except—yes, you've guessed it—that boy. He had been warned, all right. So there wasn't that excuse. Someone had gone specifically down to his part of the beach to warn him; he'd heard the call from shore, and seen the fin pointed out. There could be no mistake. The fin must have been quite distinct from where he swam, and not too far away either. But he continued to swim, quite indifferent, and even to float unconcerned on his back, rocking in the swell with just his head and the tips of his feet visible from shore. There wasn't any apparent bravado about it. He was just indifferent— to the people shouting from shore, to the cruising fin. (The shark by this time had stopped its parallel run along the shore, and was now swimming indecisively, in widening circles.)

'It's that Garland boy again,' a voice behind me revealed. There were some woeful mutterings, but I couldn't get the gist of what was said. Only that the boy was known, and evidently had some local reputation.

Anyway the scene was set and sharp for the next five minutes—the patrolling fin, the indifferent boy. Then he swam back to the beach, quite unhurried, and picked up his towel and walked away with never a glance towards any bystanders. I sensed some disappointment that the shark hadn't attacked after all. It wasn't just some unsatisfied lust for sensation. The boy seemed in part its cause. Clearly he isn't liked.

'That's the one,' someone observed. 'The boy I was telling you about.'

Which made it no clearer, for me. I stayed longer, hoping to overhear something precise, but with no luck. It was incredible how the day had changed. How a bright and friendly shore had become a brink of menace. Everything was the same—the sky and sea were still blue and unflawed—and yet nothing was the same. We weren't even conscious of the growing warmth of the sun. So long as that fin, that design for death, remained out there. The crowd thinned down, bathers dressing and departing, and soon I gave up the vigil too.

I think I shall forgo my usual swim at high tide today.

Later . . . I must have been sitting here for an hour or more, the afternoon slipping away, and not writing a word.

Later still . . . The bush crowds close to this cottage, and through my window I can just glimpse strips of the Pacific between the trees and ferns. Marvellously peaceful. No one ever calls. I could die here and it would probably be weeks before anyone knew. I really must make an effort of will and end this letter. It's not got anywhere and it's not going anywhere. My lunch is hours overdue besides. Perhaps I'll try bacon and eggs in the frying-pan again. I'm not the most enterprising of cooks, as well you know. But I have only to please myself now, after all.

It's so quiet, so damn quiet here.

Does my life sound eventful? If so, it's only because everything is rich in event for the voyeur. Take the birds I've been watching in the trees outside. But no, never mind. I call quits.

With love and much respect,

Tony

SIX

She can't account for it even now. Any more than she can account for why she doesn't force the issue. It is surely time.

But she closes the door of the shack, leaving Ted to himself—at least to his uneasy morning doze upon the couch—and emerges in the clean warmth of the sun. Her body needs it. Sometimes she feels she is only alive in summer.

Which may account for Ted, she isn't sure. It began in winter.

Jean follows the path which winds through tall native manuka, much of it stark and black with some fatally alien blight, and then down to the shore. Her thong sandals flip-flap on the hard dry earth. In sheltered places the heat is thick.

Her five-to-seven-o'clock affairs, her city flat as stopover between job and suburban home. No mystery there. There were enough affairs like that. Quite enough, she once decided, well before Ted came along. So why Ted?

No, she can't account for it, though she can remember. He hardly stood apart when she first saw him, at one of her own parties. There were a few strangers among the usual lame dogs. Ted was one of several. She couldn't, afterwards, recollect who brought him, if anyone did. He might just have wandered in by accident. She never asked. How did she acquire people anyway? Possibly the truth is that people have always acquired her. As mother confessor, patroness, mistress. She has always had a distinctly impressive number of possibilities, besides having money. And she always feels that accidental: the consequence of some fifty thousand acres of high frost-hardened mountainside she has never seen, sufficient to inspire guilt in itself. Her otherwise childless parents, heirs of both guttered pioneer hope and a certain genteel greed, sold out the sheep station for a good price before she was born, and made a number of solid investments. So the money exists, now they are dead, quite independently of her. If anything, in fact, she seems its appendage. Astonishing, really, that all the hope, all that once bold ambition, has dwindled to—well, to her. In this graceless shack, on a ramshackle island, it becomes even more unreal. She has never needed to work, though she has on occasion. She has never really needed to do anything with her life, though she sometimes tries. Certainly she can use the money, or be used on its account. She has more than once put up money to publish books of poetry she doesn't like, or bought paintings she doesn't want. Not just because people, their personalities, intervene. Not just because the poet is attractive, or the painter pitiful; or because she has a sympathetic ear. She likes to be needed, true; often needs to be needed. But only up to a point. It seems she has spent most of her adult life trying to locate that point, define it precisely, so that she can peer around and see what lies beyond. If anything does. What if there is nothing? That sometimes frightens her.

Younger she was no more attractive than she is now, though her body has always been sturdy and handsome enough for its purpose, and a certain vitality and interest in experience have made it as accessible as any. She has long prided herself on lack of illusions. She doesn't need them for stability, as she does company. Better a life crowded with people, even if largely lame, than one swarming with phantom hopes. They have been better than nothing, these people, even if not much more. Travel, when young, was one attempt at escape not only from them but from the self she was to them. But travel didn't amount to much either. Highlights were fitful, company seldom adequate, and at times the lack appalling. And she felt vulnerable. So she returned to her place in the world, her country, her friends, her cocoon.

And of course things were different. She knew they would be, if not how. The young hopefuls who once shuttled through her life were no longer young or hopeful. They were already resigned to their defeats. Their few successes had evaporated, leaving them the more bitter. They could blame everything, virtually, except themselves: their times, on occasion; their friends and enemies, sometimes; and most often their country, the country which so crudely and obstinately refused to acknowledge them. (That country which had so capriciously and unfairly endowed her.) They were in unspectacular jobs, married, coaxing children methodically into the same world which had failed them, building hedged homes in the suburbs.

Her flat remained a refuge. People still dropped in at times, but never for long now. Once they might have stopped a night, a week, a month. Now it was usually an hour or two. Just enough time to talk out their troubles and flee back to their apparently unrewarding lives again.

Those lives, then, became her burden. One which never grew lighter.

She once dreamed their dreams. Now she suffered their nightmares. She indulged, humoured, consoled, lent money she expected never to see again. She frequently took them back into her bed, but they seldom seemed to find anything they were looking for; at least anything they had lost there. She almost never saw the inside of their homes, though she occasionally met their wives. For they were sometimes displayed at her parties.

Not that she gave many parties any more, or even enjoyed them much. It was more or less just an attempt to keep the machinery of her life turning over, lest it rust from disuse. And she could never admit surprises.

Ted was one. He had a strong face.

She kicks off her sandals, drops her towel to the sand, unbuttons and tosses away her shirt. There are few people along the shore, in either direction. She has sufficient of the beach to herself. Most holidaymakers have gone; there are only a few stragglers and weekenders now. And the residents, of course, like a thin parasite growth on the tough texture of the island.

Today she has the sense of an island, something rare, a sense of the Pacific. It may be the weather partly, the clarity of the day. And it may be because she is alone, because she has lost Ted to sleep. Most days, even if he is not with her, she is aware of him uncomfortably close. She considers everything she does, everything she sees, in terms of what he may think or feel. She might have dozed on the couch beside him. Instead, escaped, she feels free. And has a glimpse of her own identity again, as if sun and sea air can restore it, or at least partially heal.

She is no longer sure what he means to her anyway. Almost all she knows for sure is the knowledge her body has, and she has begun to distrust it on that account.

A man near middle age, perhaps close to her own, comes walking along the beach. He is youthfully and fashionably dressed, in tapered blue slacks, American-style sports shirt and pointed shoes; casually dressed, but too much so for this island, too conspicuously neat. His face is rather eroded and wrinkled, though hardly by weather; the face of a leathery and sunless satyr. She hasn't seen him before, but he looks at home. In the sense, perhaps, that he seems indifferent to his surroundings. Indifference is in the easy gait of his lanky body, in his pale eyes and colourless face, even in the cigarette he smokes. It is an indifference she can identify, understand, even at times crave. His gaze makes room for her, but without apparent interest; she returns his stare serenely. He walks on, and she moves deeper into the water.

Ted's eyes were frankly appraising. She rather liked that. She was no longer used to men with confidence in themselves. Her own fault. She could not deny that. Her chosen way, her chosen life. What was she afraid of?

'A cool customer,' she observed to someone after first seeing him. 'Who is he?'

She was answered only with facts, and they were unimportant, no answer at all. It seemed he worked in some place or other, was married to some woman or other, was known by some people or other. Hardly worth listening to the recital. Later she fastened on a couple of stray opinions. One was that he'd shown great promise when young in several directions, the other was that he was now something of a genius in advertising. This troubled her. It did not seem the prescription for a happy man.

He turned up at her flat with other people again and again, though he paid scant attention to these evidently random acquaintances. This worried her too. What was he after, then? What did he want? It was inconceivable to her that he shouldn't want something. Other people seemed always to mirror her own dissatisfaction. Was he to be the same? On the other hand she couldn't tolerate the thought of another lame dog. She wished she could dismiss him as such.

The trouble was she couldn't, not even when he began to arrive at the flat alone. Hardly the act of a wholly contented man, but she didn't ask questions. She didn't want to ask questions, though they scratched within her at first. She wanted to accept face value for the first time in her life. It was too predictable otherwise. If she had to start again, what better way than trust? Trust, whatever else might be said, was the most attractive of all varieties of innocence.

Plainly he didn't look for sympathy; he appeared quite self-sufficient, as if he had everything he wanted. But he did look for possession, which almost certainly meant he hadn't. She had no objection, since she seldom had anyway, but she found afterwards she could still examine her response with mild curiosity. She wasn't quite as lost in the affair as she might have hoped. But she could try.

When he offered to leave his wife, then insisted, she was surprised but not alarmed. 'I was going to, anyway,' he said in that sure crisp way, become familiar.

She coped the only way she knew. 'We'll make a clean break,' she said. 'It's no use persisting like this.' When he hesitated, she added, 'You can find another job later. Anyway they tell me you're in demand. It shouldn't be difficult. As for me, I rather like the idea of getting clear. No problem there. I'm not needed, not really.'

She saw, in fact, an end to need. He had a strong face.

She drifts on her back in the water and watches the gulls high overhead. The cool of the ocean invades her body. She sighs.

The first thing was that shack, their refuge. She imagined he might share her pleasure in making something of it. Naturally she could have afforded better, but that wasn't the point. The point was that she didn't want to take advantage, any more than she had ever liked her money to be obtrusive. But his dismay was plain. He never said anything. And still says nothing. She has the impression he may be humouring her, for the time being at least, for the summer. Perhaps a reasonable response.

At the beginning she made it plain that it was up to him now. He could arrange his separation and divorce however he liked. In the meantime they would stay here. When things were clear, they would move back to the city. She would prefer no problems when they moved back.

He saw the point. He wrote letters. Once or twice he tripped back to the city.

Then, nothing. Still, it has been easier to wait, with the warmer weather. The only real problem is that she is involved now, something unforeseen. Perhaps it is their isolation. And it seems to have coincided with Ted's restlessness. At first he was relaxed enough on the island. Though he maintained a sardonic distance from their environment, he was easy company.

The first visible change came that afternoon she found him brooding, head in hands, at the kitchen table. He didn't look up when she appeared. She set down her purchases from the store, removed her dripping raincoat. Outside, the rain still gusted.

'What's wrong?' she asked.

He looked up finally. His face for the first time appeared vulnerable.

'Nothing,' he said. 'Just thinking.'

'Worried?'

'In a way.'

'Oh?'

He didn't seem inclined to enlighten her further. She hung up her raincoat and went to the stove.

'I feel I ought to do something with my life, or ought to have done something with it,' he said at last. 'It seems to have got away from me. I've done nothing with it.'

Either she couldn't understand or she hadn't heard right. She looked at him with disbelief.

'I was under the impression you'd done a fair amount with it already,' she observed. 'You seem to have been capable of—'

'That wasn't what I meant,' he snapped.

She knew that, of course. She was simply afraid of what he meant. It was not as if she hadn't heard declarations of despair like it before.

'It's just the day,' she offered. 'This depressing rain. It's got you down.'

'No,' he said. 'Not at all. It even helps a little.'

'Well, then . . .' She was baffled and dismayed.

'I've had time to think lately. I really ought to thank you for giving me the chance.'

'Anything to oblige,' she said with forced cheer. She really couldn't stand much more.

'Better seeing what I'm worth now than later,' he announced.

'Then what is it,' she asked, and faltered, 'what is it you want to do with yourself?'

'Just give me a chance,' he said.

She was apparently doing that, all right. She turned back to the stove and wondered how she might busy herself and postpone thought indefinitely. Lest she raced across the room to him, perhaps, in haste to console. After all, she had lived the scene before, the cues were clear. It just wasn't true, she told herself; and almost believed it.

The next day, though, he seemed reasonably normal. But he had hardened, as though ashamed, and went for a moody walk. She wasn't deceived. Did everything she touch turn lame? If so, how was it she managed to cripple?

She watched his face.

She rolls over, kicks herself forward, begins the swim back to shore. She rides a small wave into the shallows and wades out to her towel and shirt. She dries herself, sits down, and wonders if Ted is awake now, if he is on his way to join her. It is, after all, a day to be enjoyed. There hasn't been an abundance of such days this summer. And there may not be many more. She buries her face in the towel. The sun is soothing on her shoulders.

At war within himself, he grows more brutal. Yet his eyes and mouth seem accessible now, especially in sleep. In more ways than one it is clear how much he needs her. At times she watches in wonder at her own creation. His love-making has changed. Often he still takes her with an arrogant disgust. But this only seems to heighten the breathless tenderness of other encounters. In these her surrender is equally total, as if she cannot see an end.

'When are we going to get out of this place?' he has asked.

'It's rather up to you. I've made that clear.'

'I'm doing my best. Can't you trust me?'

'Of course. I do. Have I suggested otherwise?'

Too late; too late to mend now. The damage was done when she pulled him from the life in which he was sure. Now it is just a matter of hanging on, and hoping. She does a great deal of both. She has reason to be confident, after all. If she cannot do without him, he most certainly cannot do without her either, the way things are.

She wakes to the shouting. She can't tell how long she has slept; she guesses an hour or two. And Ted isn't beside her. He hasn't come down to the beach with a book, as he usually does on sunny days, to read while she sunbathes. She sits up in wild fright, brushing sand from her face, and sees people running and calling out along the shore. Then she sees the fin. And the bathers in flight. Though long out of the water herself, perfectly safe, she feels an inward shiver. The fin is so abrupt and exact in its menace. She rises, pulling on shirt and sandals, hanging the towel across a shoulder. Then she turns her back on the sea and hurries along the winding path through the manuka.

The door of the shack is shut. She remembers leaving it open. She pushes it and advances perhaps a yard inside. There is nothing left to show he has ever been there, not even a note. By now he is across the island on a bus, or seaborne on his way to the city.

She has often wondered what might be found beyond need. Now she can see. A room recently painted, a table and two chairs, a fresh print on the wall, an empty couch, some unwashed breakfast dishes.

Jean sits down slowly, as if deciding to wait for something. Down on the beach the shouting has stopped.

SEVEN

There are others.

At the moment Frank Yakich is fishing in sheltered water near the tip of the northern headland of Te Hianinu Bay, more than a mile from the beach. His catch this morning has been fair. And the commotion ashore has of course passed him by. He pulls in his last net and is about to start his small launch for home when he observes the approaching fin and counts himself lucky. Sharks have often holed his nets. Frank is not a worrying man, but his nets are precious. Dogfish are one thing, full-sized sharks another. Though more or less retired, Frank makes a modest living from supply of fresh fish to islanders incapable of fishing for themselves. Life is good to him, now that he has left the trawlers, and in his terraced backyard he grows grapes for his own wine. He cannot imagine living any other way but the way he has, and does. He has caught enough this morning to rest up for a day or two, if he likes, but chances are he will be out in the launch again tomorrow, because he likes it.

He throws a lever, the engine throbs, the launch kicks abruptly through the water. He sits at the rudder, rolling a cigarette, and when he looks up again he sees with amazement the sea creature leap near his bow. It is all too swift for his mind to register. Then, with the second shining leap, so close he feels the spray on his face, he understands. That fin. Not shark, but dolphin. And a playful one too, following him in, entertained by the engine. He rises in excitement. So too does the dolphin, seemingly, in still another leap. But this time frighteningly close to the boat. Frank shouts in dismay, for care. Then he sees his own absurdity and smiles. In fact he all but applauds as the dolphin flashes and flies around his craft, weaving, diving, ahead and then behind. A light touch on the rudder and the dolphin swings back to him like a yo-yo. Bloody marvellous, he tells himself, already soaked by the dolphin's spray; he has never had a morning quite like it. He slows, the dolphin slows. He turns, the dolphin turns. He begins to circle, but now it is the dolphin's time to tease. It vanishes entirely, speeding beneath the sea, to crash out of the water some distance away. For a moment Frank is afraid he is going to lose his company. But with a flick of its body the dolphin is riding beside him again, so close he could almost reach and touch. Frank sheds sixty of his sixty-four years and laughs like a child on a stony shore of Dalmatia. He and this dolphin seem in a sympathy so complete that they might have been the last two creatures in the world; or the first.

Experimenting, he cuts the engine. The dolphin appears to twitch with disappointment—or amusement?—and then circles. Frank watches with his breath quick in his throat. He feels sure it is circling closer. Then it is, beyond doubt, until it is inches from the craft. It touches at last. There is a rubbing sound. Back and forward, almost affectionate.

It is not me at all, Frank decides. It is the damn boat. The damn sound. I am nothing to it, nothing. Bloody cheek.

With ego wounded, he almost starts the launch homeward, into the bay. Then he sees humour in the thing and laughs again. The dolphin is still there, rubbing. He reaches into the water, seeking to inform the creature of his presence, and his hand makes contact with its coarse skin. It is as surprising to him, this coarseness, as his touch is to the dolphin. The creature swerves away. But after a time, perhaps reassuring itself, it glides to the launch again for fresh contact. Frank accepts the rebuff.

Then try an oar, he thinks. If it's a tickle you want.

The oar becomes an extension of his arm since the dolphin is now cautiously rubbing forward. It accepts the sharp edge of the oar with a faint flutter, then with growing interest, until at length it leaves the boat itself alone.

I'll be damned, Frank says to himself.

It is a long time since he has felt delight, or achievement, so great. For now he is actually nursing the dolphin back within reach. It is following the oar, turning, rolling belly upwards and over again. And cocking its head queerly. He could swear the thing is gazing at him, sizing him up. He pulls in the oar, puts a hand on the dolphin's flank, and this time is not rebuffed. He cannot quite believe it, for he knows no one else will. He begins to stroke.

Dear God, he thinks. All these years and I make friends with a bloody fish.

Harry Green is walking in his garden. It is his third such walk today. He stoops now and then to some plant he might have neglected earlier. By the end of the day, certainly, he will have missed nothing. Not one new bud, fruit or flower will have gone unseen. Not even the fast feelers of the passion-fruit vine will have escaped him. He pauses before the glowing bells of hibiscus, meditates upon the cool colours of Japanese fuchsia, examines the rich flare of his roses, sees how the young banana trees are unfurling tall leaves in the sun, bends to the fresh green of some new plants. It seems they have taken. He sighs to himself, another battle won.

Forty years a farmer on high bleak land which sometimes caught snow in winter, Harry indulged his passions only by growing grass and raising sheep; climate, soil and economics left little room for more. There was no satisfaction in that life for him, no warmth, no variety. When winter gales boomed against the farmhouse, he slept fitfully through long nights and dreamed of gardens in the sun. The years of rain and wind, mud and grass, and stinking sheep seemed a penance he must observe to earn his natural life. Then, when he saw his chance —a place on an island where bananas grew—he sold up the farm and left. Now he is owner of the old Bella Vista guest house in Te Hianinu Bay, but less interested in guests than garden. For his first two or three years the Bella Vista was empty of guests most of the year, in season taking the overflow from other places. Now it is empty of guests all the year. Harry tired of having his plants torn and lawns trampled. He pointed out to his wife that they could afford to do without this inconvenience. Anyway he has as good as retired from the world, if he or his heart was ever really in it. He never had much use for other people and hasn't now, though he has opinions. He believes in castration for criminals, healthy discipline for delinquents, painless extermination for the unfit and insane. He also believes nothing would do the world more good than another decent war. Harry has been in one war and knows perfectly well that everything has gone soft since. For proof he only needs to look around, like anyone with eyes to see. He might have gone into politics, if he had the time or patience, to put an end to nonsense. He might have made the world a peaceful pleasant place, fit for decent people. Instead he has his garden in the sun, and it may not after all be second-best.

This warm day, this highly coloured noon, sees Harry move with love among his plants, weeding and watering tenderly, on his patch of land beside the bright Pacific. It is the best time of year by far, the island quiet again, the holidaymakers almost gone. As if to shoo the last away, there has been the shark off shore this morning. No longer do strangers batter on the door of the Bella Vista, asking—sometimes demanding—that the place open again for guests. No longer are beach and roadside littered. No longer do transistor radios compete, or beery louts brawl or babies howl. The crenellated wooden turrets of the Bella Vista, a builder's one extravagance in a long austere life, today stand bold above the flowers and fruiting trees in the island's new calm. Harry feels prickles of pleasure in the day.

A sound attracts him. He looks up, shading his eyes. But it is only Yakich the fisherman travelling back into the bay. Something is odd, though, and he looks again before he runs inside to fetch his binoculars and shout to his wife, 'Take a look out there. Old Yakich has gone bloody mad. He's turning circles out in the bay. Or cartwheels, damn near.'

Ben Blackwood sits at his makeshift desk—an old door propped by appleboxes and stray boards—and wonders how much good he is doing the world or himself this morning by thinking about Vietnam.

It isn't as if he really knows much about Vietnam anyway. He has never been there. He isn't even sure what language is spoken. He would be hard put to convey the physical appearance of the people. Until lately he possibly couldn't have found the place on a map of the world without difficulty. And it is not as if, even now, he has gone particularly in quest of information. Almost all he knows he has learned incidentally, mainly against his will, from newspapers and radio and television. About all that is very clear is that enormous quantities of people are slaughtering, and being slaughtered, evidently on his behalf.

It almost happens to be Vietnam at random. In perverse moments of meditation he wonders if such stricken countries are losers in some cosmic lottery. For it could just as well be another place. The world seems rich in places one has difficulty finding on a map because people are dying there in sudden outrageous number. True, his present country, which now sometimes seems his own, is also difficult to find on a map—as he is only too often aware—but at least there is not the same excuse to find it. People around him may be dying, but in largely leisurely fashion, and demonstrably not because of bullet, bomb or napalm. There are no mothers sobbing and searching. There are no executions in the street, no demented refugees in flight. This, however, is no commendation, nor consolation; he feels all the more oppressed.

It is impossible, quite impossible. He can't think clearly on any subject—let alone get ahead with the story he is supposed to be writing—without slithering down again suddenly into that well-spiked trap, wherever it is and whoever is dying there. At times Vietnam seems less the name of a country than the name of an illness, some hieroglyphic which he is obliged to unriddle. Perhaps he is going out of his mind.

All evasion, of course; cynicism disguised as psychology can explain everything. Evasion. A way to backslide, pure and perfect, a way to avoid the problem of his work and life. Vietnam, he can just imagine one-time friends saying, is Ben's new escape from himself. A nice explanation, and neat. He wishes it true, in a way. He wishes it were an escape. He really doesn't want to feel physically ill at his desk every morning. He would write out his resignation from the human race, if that would help, though perhaps not in so extreme a fashion as Sheila.

'Anyway,' she said against the muffled sounds of London, 'you're the one who most needs to look after yourself. Wait and see. Things are sometimes real, Ben—really real, horribly real, beyond a joke.'

He lights a cigarette, his fifth before the blank sheet in the typewriter, and is no longer concerned about lung cancer. It is more a votive offering now, a small enough sacrifice to the blank sheet, the unwritten story. Though he can't see how his own extinction will make liquefied children solid. Or even that his story will help, if written. He rises from his desk, his limbs half atrophied, and tries to spit some of the sourness from his mouth into the fireplace. The moisture subsides and vanishes into last winter's ash. Time for a spring-clean, surely; he wishes he could do the same for his mind.

His trouble of course isn't that he is writing about Vietnam, or anything like it, but that he is not. He would if he could but he can't. Instead he is composing another fairy tale for adults, or trying to. Recognizing this, he is overwhelmed by a stark sense of his own inadequacy. He cannot connect and perhaps will never now. Forster, who once seemed so wise, mocks from his remote and cosy corner of the century.

So he begins to write after all, connecting the only way he knows how, contriving still another unpublishable Letter to the Editor. ('Dear Sir, It is time . . .') He tries again. ('Dear Sir, I cannot imagine . . .') And yet again. ('Dear Sir, May I say . . .') Worse still, but there are many sheets of paper still blank. ('Dear Sir, Get stuffed . . .')

He sits for a time with his head in his hands. Who is this almighty Sir, this plainly absurd Editor, anyway? Then he feels the peace of decision. Upright, he lights another cigarette and strikes tentatively at the typewriter.

'Dear God,' he begins, 'I feel obliged to draw your attention to certain types of anti-personnel weapons now being perfected, with considerable success, upon your people in Vietnam ..'

There is some shouting down on the beach and though he is usually vulnerable to distraction, even by a soundless fly upon the ceiling, this morning he is not.

An hour or so later the letter is finished, but he cannot think where to mail it. He literally rests upon his morning's work, dozes fitfully upon his desk. Not even the erratic engine sound beyond his window disturbs him.

By mid-afternoon most people know about Frank Yakich and the dolphin. If they have not seen, they have heard. Some of the elderly who have both seen and heard grow confused. It is even said that Frank Yakich has befriended a shark.

Late in the afternoon a half-dozen small craft, dinghies powered by outboard motors, move around the bay in search. But their occupants have to make do with sight of small fish leaping.

Some people walk the length of the beach till evening, waiting. Others watch from their open windows. No fin is sighted.

Clearly the creature is gone, a thing of the day, though some may still speak of it weeks or even months from now. By dusk Te Hianinu Bay is already beginning to sleep upon the memory.

An idiot child walks the darkening beach with his defeated mother. He breaks free of her hand, races down to the water. A wave rises around his thin ankles.

'Come back,' he cries into the night. 'Come back, shark.'

EIGHT

It was the dare game, more than anything. Though no one understands. He tried once to explain but gave up. Who could? Often he is not sure he understands either, though he has more time than anyone to think about it, and more reason.

Today more than most days. It is a year exactly, a year since it ended, since they played the game for the last time. So he lives it again from the moment he goes out into the day. This is not difficult. It is only difficult not to live again, and he has felt the day coming as if in his blood. And his parents, as though they know, have neglected to hang the new year's calendar. That is the worst thing, how much they know and how little they understand, or anyone.

At Diana's funeral he determined not to weep, with everyone watching, and didn't; he was going to choose his own time and place. If he wept before others, they might only say it was remorse.

He found he couldn't win either way. They said he was shameless. 'That kid,' they said. 'He was so damn brazen about it. He didn't even pretend to grieve when they buried her.'

The fools. What do they know? He is just seventeen, and people fairly sicken him.

But then everyone knows he killed his sister. That is the trouble, there can be no dispute. At least about that one fact. The impossible thing is that they also assume he wanted to. Which shows what they are like, really. How strange and black their minds are, and how appalling.

But after the funeral he bit upon the words he might have shouted, and finally wept almost not at all, because he forgot.

To his verdict of death by misadventure the coroner added a rider about misuse of firearms by adolescents.

He cannot remember the beginning of the game. It seemed to have been there all the time, like Diana. It was part of their growing, the excitement.

'Dare,' Diana said. And they climbed the highest tree, swam to the furthest point.

'Dare,' he said. And there was a high cliff to scale, a deep crevice to leap.

They were always evenly matched. They could never get much interested in other children, who could not compete.

Mr Garland was once a lawyer. Never a good one, perhaps because he couldn't see himself in the part, though his lawyer father could. And also because of his breakdowns. At first these were just minor eruptions of ill-health, becoming more and more frequent, along with his absences from his office. To his children he was usually remote, as though inwardly grieving for them as much as himself. He could not communicate, though he apparently tried when he reached out, rather furtively, to touch their faces with his fingertips; and then withdrew. At times he seemed almost to convey something, though neither of the children could say what. His touch was so gentle. He might have been searching for grip, lest he sank. Mrs Garland too, though she embraced.

'I want you to do whatever you want,' he said, when the subject rose, early in their lives. 'To be whatever you want.'

This caused them no thought. They already took it for granted, for nothing had ever suggested otherwise. Anyway it was too soon.

He persisted, however, as they grew, and until they understood. This was when his ill-health was becoming more frequent. It seemed he might once have wanted to be other than himself, even if why was not clear. It might not have been clear to him either, now.

He had already begun to talk oddly. At last it was as apparent in his office as in his home. When he did not talk, he sat reflective, one hand above his eyes, as if that would steady his vision. In the other hand a pipe often lay unsmoked. He was frequently found like this in his office, even the morning paper untouched on his desk. And he spent longer periods at home in a silence so complete that the children circled it, cautiously. Even his wife was tentative about invasion. Sometimes it seemed nothing else but that silence existed in the house.

The children grew, all the same. His silence did not really disturb, any more than his talk had and did. They grew, and dared. Their father's premature retirement did not shrink their natural territory, rather it was enlarged. For soon after came the shift from the country town to the island, where no one knew them, and where Mr Garland might enter his silences without distraction, or talk strangely to the gulls on beaches he walked. But actually Mr Garland improved remarkably. It might have been the sea, his walks, or the garden in which he took so great an interest. It appeared he had always wanted, more than most things, to grow gherkins and cultivate capsicums. If he still spoke strangely, it was never within earshot, never to his wife and children. And on this island, beside the Pacific, a man's small silences merged with greater.

The children sought no friends, because there was no need, and anyway none to replace. They always shared more than their birthdays. They had their fourteenth birthday the day after they came to the island, and their sixteenth the day before the thing happened. He has not celebrated his lone birthday this year, and even his parents have been careful to forget. Perhaps he will never again, since half the point is gone and half of so much else.

Friends? The trigger he pressed, he is never sure why, struck down not only Diana but even the possibility of anyone else.

Her eyes were so bright.

Mrs Garland is a woman too heavily burdened. Her hair has greyed, and her hands often start trembling without warning, though she hangs on. Her husband should have been sufficient for her lifetime. He is weight enough to carry, and has been even more. Sometimes she surprises herself, not so much in not cracking, for she does at times, but rather in finding herself still intact and alive in the mornings. Then she has to tell herself over again, so she can believe. It is still difficult. A year is too flimsy a thing, and too little to heal. Yet lately she has glimpsed, from a narrowing distance, some strangely serene region beyond despair. A cool place, coolly coloured, where she may rest. And a place which taunts as much as tempts, for she cannot accept its promise and perhaps will not. What she has begun to accept now is that the loss of Diana is something beyond repair, and that David's condition is possibly not. Yet that does not make her any the less powerless. Even her husband is shocked into a coherence sufficient to see the problem, and sometimes share. The trouble is that David has nothing to say, even if they have. They cannot even begin.

And certainly not this morning, of all. She and her husband both try to be normal at the breakfast table, and both fail. The date seems distinct on their faces. David sits motionless, not eating. Then he walks out.

They can only wait now. At least he does not have the rifle. It is locked away, though it has been promised again. To her relief he has not asked for it. It is possible he does not know the day, though she does not doubt it.

They carry the new rifle in turn across the scrubby hills to the south of Te Hianinu Bay. Near them, the land dips steeply to rocky shore and twists of sand. The grass beneath their bare feet is moist and springy after rain. But the morning sun is already beginning to dry. A rabbit bobs in the distance, between clumps of grass on a ridge. He fires experimentally and the shot startles another, nearer, from hiding. He shoots and runs, shoots and runs, but in the end misses that too.

It makes the day no better. Diana is still in her queer mood.

He walks breathless back to her and hands her the rifle in silence. She snicks out the spent cartridge and snips home the bolt on a new. She offers him no word of consolation and he does not expect it. Her face has that sullen expression, fast grown familiar. She raises the rifle slantwise before her body and they begin to walk again. Soon he starts to trail, a few yards and then fifty behind, taking refuge and comfort in a mood of his own.

It is nothing new, this scene. It began before yesterday's birthday celebration, if celebration is the word. It seems Diana resents his share in her life and is determined to show it. He is perplexed and at times feels stranded. Yet they are still as much together as they have always been, and no one intrudes. What is the trouble? He may be one day nearer knowing, but just now, trailing behind, he doubts it. Today he is glad just to be clear of their birthday, and into their seventeenth year. And at least the day is perfect, too bright even for their moods to muddy. Everything is clean, dripping and shining, after the night's rain. The air seems crisp enough to eat. The sun gathers strength as they walk. He feels swamp ooze beneath his feet, then coarse grass. Spider-webs glimmer among the scrub. Shadows in the folds of the hills thin and then vanish as the sun rises higher. The scrub is salted with pale and tiny aromatic flowers. They plunge into it briefly, and he hears Diana crackling somewhere ahead.

She emerges on a rise, beside a dead tree, lifting the butt of the rifle to her shoulder and peering somewhere ahead. Her body is rigid in silhouette, as long and lean as his own. Apart from the flow of her hair and the contour of her newly risen breasts, she is certainly no less angular. He waits, tense with anticipation, quite stationary. She seems a long minute sighting in the soundless day, and he hears his own breathing. Then her finger squeezes and the rifle cracks. He knows from the sudden slump of her body that she has missed, like himself, and her bitter laugh confirms it.

Her laugh is new too. He doesn't like it, any more than he understands it. She stalks back in disgust and plants the rifle firmly in his hands.

'There,' she says. 'All yours.'

'You've got another turn,' he says. 'I had two.'

'It's not my day,' she observes, and walks on.

'Then that makes both of us,' he announces.

She does not reply. She continues to stride ahead. More in the direction of the shore than anywhere, if she has a direction. He follows with the rifle. They scramble down to a track which runs parallel to the shore, back towards Te Hianinu. Diana is frowning, as if she even worries herself. She appears to grow irritated with the track after a time, and when they near Te Hianinu she strikes up an abrupt slope of Hau hill. It is an almost perpendicular climb with next to no vegetation for hand-holds. She seems not to care that he is hindered by the rifle, and it may even be her intention to leave him behind. Though he finds this idea, when he considers it, as inconceivable as ever. He slings the rifle tight and awkward over his shoulder, and follows again. Behind is a four-hundred-foot drop to rocks and sea. His persistence in following is justified when Diana pauses after a few yards, looks back, and gives a tight smile. 'Dare,' she says, and everything is all right again. She waits until he is level, and the race begins. At times, as they claw their way higher, they sway out and away from the hill and then swing back to its unyielding surface again. His heart thumps, his breath hurts in his throat. He keeps pace with Diana, despite the rifle. Small rocks rattle away behind, the sound diminishing, down to the sea. Sweat runs into his eyes like acid, and the sun burns on his neck. Then, pausing for new grip on the split flesh of the hill, he looks sideways and sees Diana's face.

She may be dying. That is his first thought. She looks in agony. But this, whatever the cause, doesn't make her effort any the less intense. For the two things appear entirely separate, the agony and the effort, though she may be trying to involve one with the other, for all he can tell, but without success or hope of it.

He is so startled, Diana gains. Now the hill seems incidental, like their contest, like the dare. Diana has it on her own.

They finish in a cleft, a small plateau, some way below the summit of Hau hill. Diana crawls on to it first, and he is not far behind. She rolls on her back and looks up at the sky, breathing painfully. He unslings his rifle before collapsing, and it rests between them. There is none of the old excitement or laughter, and certainly no triumph claimed. Their effort ends like lead on that plateau. Her first words are leaden too.

'What a waste of time,' she breathes. 'Always was.'

He cannot argue, though he can puzzle.

'Why don't you hate me?' she asks. 'You really ought.'

Never mind, he tells himself. Stay quiet and it will pass. It has always passed before.

'What's the matter? Anyone would think you didn't have a tongue. Come on. Say something. Just to prove you're there.'

He is, but still slack with exhaustion. He is also afraid.

She sits up. 'Are you really there?'

'I am,' he says. 'For God's sake.' He pauses. 'Now forget it, leave it alone.'

'Prove it,' she says. 'Prove that you're there. If you can.' Her voice is harder, tighter, with each word. She is still breathing fast. 'Go on. Dare.'

It sounds mockery, unashamed, of all that they have been and still fitfully are. And there is cruelty too, as if she wishes to rend. He is very still.

'Dare,' she repeats.

Again he refuses a reaction.

'Scared?' she says. 'Let's see.'

She flips up the rifle and he is looking into its thin barrel, just three feet away. He does not move. She plays experimentally with the safety catch.

'Still not there?' she says. 'If you aren't there, if you don't exist, there's nothing to stop me pulling this trigger. Is there?'

'That's up to you,' he observes. He buries his face in his arms again, but there is tension in the back of his neck now, where the rifle is probably pointed. After all, Diana is strange to the point of menace now. And her finger may slip. He prefers not to provoke. 'Please yourself.'

'Then you are scared,' she pronounces. 'Dare. Go on.'

She has hardly said this when he springs, under the rifle, so it becomes useless and awkward in her hands. It falls aside and he pins her arms. Yet this is by no means conquest. She can still resist, and does. Her body heaves beneath him and he rocks. His grip grows fiercer and, pushing down with all the pressure he can summon, he tries to hold her still. His face is close to hers, though he does not really see her. He may have the advantage in position now, but they are quite as evenly matched as they have been. She looks almost pleased as they struggle. Then her teeth bite into his shoulder, something he hasn't counted on, and he goes wild with the pain. He loses his advantage, tumbles, and they are both struggling loose on the ground. But soon, with their limbs threaded brutally and bodies impacted, it is near enough to deadlock. She smiles oddly and goes limp. He is alert for a ruse.

'So you are there,' she says. 'You did prove it.'

His shoulder still hurts and perhaps bleeds. It is hard to forgive. He doesn't reply.

'It wasn't so bad, either, was it?'

Her face is near his again, and her breath comes sharply. Her eyes are bright and looming. He can't avoid them.

'I could bite again.'

'I expect you could,' he says with disgust.

'Don't tell me it didn't surprise you.'

'You surprise me. That's all.'

'At last,' she sighs. Her eyes roll with mock gratification. 'At last.'

His anger thickens in his chest. 'What do you mean?'

'I want to surprise you. I thought I'd never find a way.'

'Well, you have,' he says bluntly. 'You pleased now?'

'I might be. It depends.' Her voice is cool.

'How does it depend?'

'On how surprised you are. Or how afraid.'

He tries to laugh. 'And what am I supposed to be afraid of?'

'You ought to know.'

She is entirely inert now, and still smiling. Again he tries to laugh. It becomes more difficult.

'You're afraid of me,' she adds. 'That's all.'

'So how do I show I'm not?'

'That would be telling. But go on. Dare.'

Her teeth go into his hand this time, and he leaps. 'See,' she says. 'Scared.'

Now they are both seeking pain, almost by way of relief. Their bodies bend grotesquely. There might be some other end, if he can see it. 'Afraid,' she says into his ear. 'Afraid. Afraid.'

His heart is explosive, and his lungs. He jolts her head back onto the ground again and again, so her teeth rattle, but she still looks indifferent. There seems no way to penetrate her taunting.

Until he wrestles free, and has the rifle pointed in her face. It appears just to happen. Her breath comes raggedly, and her eyes are bright. He has never seen them so bright.

'Afraid of that too,' she says. 'Go on, then. Dare.'

She jerks back from the shot and twitches. But he does not remember much of that. His last intact memory is of her face, in the instant it happens. She does not look afraid. She looks relieved.

He hears the shouts from shore, sees the onlookers pointing. The fin cruising in the sea seems an answer to the question the day has posed him, an answer to himself.

For the first time in a year he says the word.

'Dare,' he whispers, and feels peace. He swims still further out from shore, and floats idly on his back, though at any moment the teeth may strike. He is more than ready.

He and the shark have the sea to themselves now. None will dare intrude, and the people on shore are silent. He has felt the day must hold something, and now he knows. He may know too how Diana felt, in that instant, for they are sharing again. He wonders if his eyes are as bright. All things seem to flow together, tributaries to the one stream, and he feels relief.

He cannot see the fin, and shuts his eyes as he floats, lest he might. He wants nothing to distract. For in the excitement of his body he seems to understand Diana at last, if too late, and himself; he may really begin to know.

But nothing happens, nothing.

Apparently nothing will, no matter how long he waits. At first he is unwilling to believe this, but time offers proof. The anticipation in his flesh subsides, and all illusion leaks away into the passing minutes. He is emptied again, and solid.

He is simply floating in the sea. It might be any day.

'Dare,' he repeats in a whisper, but it is no use, the challenge is gone, and there is not even himself to hear. He might just have hurled the word as something fragile against a wall, to shatter. It no longer has meaning.

He persists, though, until this is quite clear. Then he rolls over. The fin is distant, and most onlookers have shifted down the beach. He swims slowly back to shore.

He supposes his parents relieved the day is past.

NINE

Next morning Frank Yakich has company again. This time the beach is crowded, and binoculars flash here and there. Children, to get a better view, perch high in the limbs of the pohutukawa along the shore. The sea is calm, and there is no surf at all. The dolphin performs to the tune of Frank's engine and later, when he silences the launch, allows itself to be petted with oar and mop. Frank manages to nurse the creature close into shore so that everyone, in the end, can see it quite plain, from tail to humorous bottle-nose. At one stage it glides, independent of the launch, into shallow water, moving its dark body with gentle undulations. But when a child splashes gleefully into the water, to greet it, the creature streaks back to Frank and his launch. The incident ends in sharp reprimand and childish tears. Soon after the dolphin heads out into open water with a last flick of its tail.

Ben Blackwood, who has spent most of the morning composing improbable correspondence, and learns of the dolphin late, races down to the shore, trips on a pohutukawa root, falls breathless on the sand.

Jean walks slowly home. On the way she passes, without really seeing, the dapper middle-aged man she noticed the day before. He is still, for the most part, watching the sea. She is too self-absorbed to hear and acknowledge his muttered greeting.

From his vantage-point high on the side of Hau hill, David Garland flings angry stones towards the sea. It all seems, from where he sits, to have happened in a quiet strange world, like something at the wrong end of a telescope. It also seems, after yesterday, a bad joke.

'The newspapers are coming,' Harry Green announces. 'They just rung me up to ask was it true.'

'The bloody thing,' Frank Yakich is telling people. 'The damn bloody thing. It was grinning at me. What do you think of that?'

Professor Thomson continues, too late for dead low tide, on his morning walk. Behind him, not far, is a faint clack-clacking of beads.

They pass the pub, filling up with noisy drinkers.

'You saw it,' a small voice says. It is a statement, not a question.

'Yes,' he agrees, but dares not turn. 'I did.'

'You saw it,' she repeats. And seems content.

He walks some way further before he decides to speak again. He is almost at the rocks before he turns to confront the girl. But he has not noticed that the beads have stopped clacking behind him. The girl is gone.

'Saw the golphin,' says the child.

'Dolphin,' says his sister.

'Big golphin,' says the child. 'Big, big golphin.'

'Dolphin,' says his sister. She wipes his nose. 'You saw the dolphin.'

'Golphin eats people,' announces the child. 'Golphin gobbles people all up.'

'A dolphin does not.'

'Golphin does.'

'Sharks eat people. Dolphins don't. Dolphin, not golphin.'

'Golphin,' says the boy happily. 'I seen the golphin gobbling all up.'

'Big bastard,' says the old man at the bar, filling his pipe.

'Seen bigger,' says the barman with the tattooed arm. 'Around the ships. Some so big, in the war, we thought they was submarines.'

'Funny,' the old man says. 'Wonder what he's looking for here?'

'Same as we're all looking for, I expect,' the barman says. 'A bit of fun, to pass the time.'

'Good luck to him. I can think of better places to swallow the anchor.'

'And worse,' the barman says. He moves on to another drinker.

'Funny,' the old man says into his beer. But he doesn't smile.

'Stuff me,' says the fat honeymooner. 'I seen everything now.' 'Just think,' says his wife, as he gets into bed with her. 'Just think, darling. Our first dolphin. Our very first.'

He grunts into her shoulder.

'It's almost like it's specially for us,' she continues. 'Don't you think so, Bill?'

He grunts again.

'Perhaps it's a sign,' she says. 'A sign that we'll be very happy.'

Bill soon appears to be happy enough. Shortly afterwards he is snoring.

The idiot child tries to run down to the sea, but this time his mother is prepared. She catches his hand and holds him back. Tears run down his face.

'Come back, shark,' he calls.

'He came back once,' his mother says. 'What more do you want? You can't have everything.'

'Come back, shark,' the child calls. 'Come back.'

Excitement trembles along the beach for an hour or more afterwards. An old crippled lady, supported by sticks, is helped down to the sand.

'And you say it was here?' she says. 'Just a little while ago?'

'Right here,' she is assured.

'Then I'll wait,' she says. 'It might come back. I might see it.'

They help her sit down in shade. Her sticks rest beside her useless legs. But she looks in the wrong direction. She is also blind.

'And you made friends with this fish?' says the reporter, who has flown out from the city by amphibian plane. 'Would it be correct to say that?'

'No,' says Frank Yakich. 'I wouldn't say that at all.'

'No?'

'No,' says Frank. And leaves it at that.

'Then what would you say?' asks the reporter with impatience.

'I don't know what is to say. I think I would say only is bloody marvellous thing to see.'

'But you made friends with this fish? Isn't that so?'

'I would not say that neither.'

'No?'

'No. In first place dolphin is not true fish. Is mammal, like us. Is warm blood creature, not cold. In second place I do not make friends with this mammal, to speak true.'

'No? Then just what did you do?'

'Nothing. The bloody thing make friends with me.'

The reporter takes a note. 'Just one more thing, then. Would you say it's likely to come back again?'

Frank shrugs. 'How should I know? I am not God.'

'I realize that. But your opinion?'

'My opinion is if bloody thing comes back, it comes back. My other opinion is if bloody thing doesn't come back, it doesn't. I just tell you. I am not God. This bloody thing make friends with me, then maybe is gone for good. How should I know?'

The reporter has very little by way of colour and character, apart from a dour Dalmatian fisherman. He also has very little by way of fact, aside from the actual dolphin, which no one seems able to describe clearly anyway. Perhaps there isn't much to the story after all. Possibly a bright paragraph or two; a one-day wonder.

'Just one last thing. You sure it was a dolphin?'

'I think I know shark when I see one,' Frank observes, 'and is just too bad if this is one.' He holds up his right hand. 'I have this hand to show. This hand that touched it.'

'Those people down there look like they're going to hang round all day,' Harry Green announces. 'They been coming in from all over the island. All people want, these days, is something to gawk at. To take their mind off themselves.'

His wife, busy in the kitchen of the echoing Bella Vista, says nothing.

'A fat chance they got of seeing it anyway,' he adds. 'I bet the thing won't be back.'

'What makes you say that?' asks his tired wife.

'If I was a fish,' Harry proposes, 'I could think of better things to do.'

'Better things?'

'Better things than coming here to be gawked at, by this lousy lot. I'd keep well clear. When you think of what it's got out there, down there.' Harry pauses for breath, words defeating him, and sees himself flit through the deeps of the sea, swift among flashes of fish and cords of coloured coral in a dappled light, curving past the mellow fruit of

underwater gardens, everything so quiet. 'If that fish has any sense . . .'
   'Perhaps it hasn't,' says his wife.

I should really have posted this yesterday [*he continues*] and now I'm
glad I couldn't quite bring myself to. I can add a footnote about our
little comedy. That shark yesterday wasn't. I mean it wasn't a shark. It's
a fantastically tame dolphin. It's been playing round the beach this
morning, with a fisherman, and everyone on the beach to see. Since
then people from all over the island have been parading—or limping,
hobbling, creeping—up and down the beach in hope it reappears. Be
terrible if it doesn't. Though I've been keeping my distance since I
came to live here, as I've said, I find myself quite involved emotionally
with these poor old dears and the children too. What I mean is, for
their sake and my own peace of mind, I hope the damn thing comes
back. This has really made my day. I'm afraid it's even taken
precedence over my other interests. That boy, for instance—he seems
to be well clear of the beach today. Yet yesterday he was so enthusiastic
about swimming he was actually prepared to share the water with
what we thought to be a shark. The Professor and his little camp-
follower were about this morning, but I lost them in the crowd. I did
see him later by himself. He always looks so perplexed and down in
the mouth I feel I should speak to him and ask if he knows his way
home. But as I say, I never speak to anyone here, except from
necessity. Isolation may be making me a little strange, but I feel I am
beginning to see things with what appears a new clarity. For all the
use that is; God knows. I'm beginning to feel I don't even exist—at
times. To confirm this, I've just remembered an incident on the beach
this morning, when I did actually speak to someone. Well, at least said
'good morning' politely. No response. I might have been invisible. I
hope I don't really have to resort to lengthy conversation to prove I'm
not. Well, the beach tempts. I can't resist returning to see if anything
has happened again down there. Perhaps our island comedy isn't
finished yet. And I really must post this letter today. I'll feel better
when it's out of my life. Or should I say even better. Amazing how
much more interesting I find the world.

On his way home from the beach Ben Blackwood's feet grow suddenly
and incredibly heavy outside a house where a radio plays a news

broadcast. He really wishes to hurry past, but cannot. It is largely because of escape from things like this—news broadcasts, newspapers, television—that he lives on Motutangi. So he can work, or try to. He doesn't have radio or television and it is months since he bought a newspaper. It seems a less expensive refuge than the liquor he once used in quantity. And also less rewarding? He isn't sure. Curiosity subverts him, sensitive to the slightest chink in his shell. He eavesdrops on news broadcasts. And in the grocery store his eyes dart involuntarily to the newspapers heaped on the counter, and the headlines.

It seems today that another city is being destroyed to save it; and half a hundred other villages and towns. A politician insists the use of nuclear weapons would be merciful and Christian.

It is reasonable, of course, and perhaps predictable that the end should begin in a place called Vietnam. It could equally well be in a place called Cuba, or Korea. All much of a muchness, all things considered. The end may as well be called Vietnam as anything; it cannot be just the name of a country again.

He continues homeward, his feet still heavy. Resignation doesn't help his work, any more than his missed sight of the dolphin. Loose stones click beneath his feet and a faint clay dust rises. He ought, he tells himself, to be content, along with most of the passively barbarian tribe to which he belongs. The technicians of terror operating on his behalf have, after all, done their best to make the world's human problems fewer within the past twenty-four hours.

He leans on the door of his cottage and it opens. He stands for a time looking at his untidy desk. He doesn't have ignorance as excuse, or even indifference. He has no excuse. But he also has nothing to say. He has nothing in fact, except his fairy tales. And even, apparently, those no longer.

He sits at his desk. Then he is certain, quite certain, he is going off his head. He starts shivering.

After a time, however, he goes to a dusty window and tries to see if anything is happening down on the beach. He doesn't want to be late next time.

Nothing is happening. The newspaper reporter flies back to the city. The crowd on the beach thins down. Harry Green, wandering his garden, feels relief.

TEN

There are, though, far more people than usual along and around the beach next morning, just in case. Again binoculars are pointed seaward, in the direction from which Frank Yakich is thought most likely to appear. Children idle and play away the time happily enough, and some soon forget why they are there. It is only the adults who grow restive. A few become quite irritable with the noise of the children, the mounting heat of the day, and grumble home. For it is another clear and warm day, the air still and the sea calm. The waves which flash up the sand are small.

When the launch is at last seen in the distance, coming into sight round the northern headland, those holding binoculars appear reluctant to reveal the truth. 'It don't look like he's got it,' a man announces finally. 'It don't look like it's with him.'

The launch grows larger, nearing the beach, until there can be no doubt. There are sighs of disappointment, mutters of disgust. 'I told you so,' declares one man.

'Then why did you come?' demands his wife.

They quarrel their way off the beach. A few of the old men head toward the pub.

Frank Yakich can be seen clearly now, in the back of the launch, holding up empty hands. He may be offering some excuse, but most people are no longer interested. Just one or two wait to meet him when he comes ashore.

'Is out there still,' he tells them. 'Is still around, all right. But today bloody thing won't come in. Maybe too tired, after yesterday.' He shrugs. 'And maybe bloody thing is fed up with me. Life must be not

75

all fun and games, even for him.'

Frank goes home with a noticeably small catch. Those who have heard his story linger for a time, looking out to sea, before they depart the beach too.

At the south end of the beach, near the rocks, are two moving figures about ten yards apart. From his place on the side of Hau hill, where he sits flinging stones into the day, the boy has a good view of the pair below. He even takes a mild interest in them, to the extent of wondering who they are, what they are about, and why they do not speak. A curious couple. What is he after, and why does she follow?

He rests flat on his belly and watches. The man slows, stops. So does the girl.

The beads stop rattling before he turns. She appears to flinch when he faces her. And then to tremble, as though about to flee, when he walks back to her. He wishes he were less tired. He seems to fight his way up through a great numbing weariness to speak, something grey and heavy. His own words, when he hears them, sound remarkably remote.

'All right,' he sighs. 'So tell me what you want. And why you ran away yesterday.'

She has nothing to say, though her lips evidently struggle.

'Tell me,' he insists.

It looks as if she may be about to cry, and her voice is small. No doubt about it, she is alarmingly odd. 'I ran away because I talked to you,' she says, as if that can explain.

He puzzles, trying to focus.

'Because you talked to me?'

'Yes.' Again the small, remote voice.

'So . . .' he begins, and stops.

She waits. Her face is quite expressionless now.

'So you're shy,' he says. 'You've been wanting to talk to me?'

'Yes,' she agrees. She looks down at her unshod feet, or at the sand. Her fingers twitch toward some part of her clothing, then fall away. 'Yes. I wanted to talk to you. And yesterday I did.'

'I see,' he says, though he does not. They seem already to have reached a dead end, and he gropes for a question. 'How old are you?' he asks, for some reason.

'Twenty,' she says, and looks up at him. 'No, eighteen. I always just say twenty. It sounds better.'

'It's old to be shy,' he observes, though for himself he cannot remember. He must have been eighteen once, it is obvious, and twenty too. Was either better? He cannot imagine now. But he tries.

'You never look as if you want to talk,' she explains carefully. 'Even when . . .' But her new courage appears to fail her.

'Yes?' he says. 'Even when?'

'When you were at the university,' she finishes quickly. 'Walking round there. I used to see you, sometimes.'

'You were there?' he says with disbelief.

She nods.

He still cannot believe it. 'You were a student? One of mine?'

She shakes her head with remarkable vigour. 'I was washing dishes, or pouring tea. In the cafeteria, you see. It was the job I had.'

He begins to relax as the mystery shrinks. Most things are explicable after all.

Then she adds, 'But I used to go to lectures too, when I had an hour. Yours, sometimes. There were so many students. No one would notice me.'

He thinks this unlikely, but does not say so.

'I would just sit there,' she goes on, 'and listen. Sometimes I would even write things down, to be like the others. So they would not notice.'

'But why?'

'So I could learn, of course. About the things I should know, and the books I should read. I didn't always understand.'

It might have been indecent exposure, and in a way is. Anyway for the moment he cannot look at her, or speak. There seems to be some obstruction in his throat which he has first to clear.

'You don't mind?' she says in dismay. 'You don't mind me telling you?'

'No,' he lies, drowning. 'It's quite reasonable for you to tell me. But what made you do it?'

'Nothing made me. Nothing. I just wanted to. But I suppose it might have been my father.'

'And who is he?'

'He was on the railways. Before.'

'Before what?' It is like a carver chipping away at wood, to find a shape inside.

'Before people said he was strange with his thinking and talking and took him away. When he came back again he fell under a train. It was an accident, and my mother got money. Everyone said it was an accident. They wanted to help.'

'But I don't see,' he begins, 'how this—'

'It was my father used to talk to me, and give me books to read. So I could understand. But I wasn't old enough. Then he went away and came back again and fell under that train. They did something to him in the hospital. He wasn't the same any more. Whatever they did to him, I don't know. He didn't talk any more. He was quiet even with me. He stopped reading before the accident, because he couldn't any more. He gave me all his books. But my mother said afterwards, after the train, there had to be an end to it, and took all the books away from me. She sold them. I've been trying to find what they were, what was in them, ever since. Sometimes I think I can remember things—like bits of music far away. And sometimes I don't think I can remember at all.' She puts a hand to her head. 'I just try.'

'And you thought we might help,' he says, 'when you took that job at the university?'

'Yes,' she agrees. 'That was why.'

'Well, it's no use coming to me now. I've finished with it.'

She nods solemnly. 'Yes, I know. I mean I was there. The day you finished. I know.'

He might have known, should have. Sweat glitters on his forehead.

'So you see,' he says hastily, 'I couldn't get you enrolled as a proper student. I'm no longer connected. I'm away from it all now. Your best course would be to get directly in touch with the university. Of course they might consider—'

'No,' she declares. 'That's not why I wanted to talk to you.'

'I don't see what else there can be,' he replies shortly. 'And I'm sure I can't help you with your father's books, wherever they are.'

He starts walking again, by way of protest. She follows, at his elbow now.

'I couldn't be a student anyway,' she explains. 'Not really.'

'No?' He begrudges her even that response, but finds he has given it.

'I left school years ago. When I was fifteen. My mother made me. She bought a house here on the island with that money she got. For a while I had nothing to do. Then I went away and got that job.'

They arrive at sudden rocks. They pause, and then he begins to scramble upwards.

'What was it you were telling us?' she asks, from behind. 'What was it?'

He struggles on to the rocks, faintly breathless, and looks down at the girl. She has begun to follow.

'I don't understand,' he says, though he is beginning.

'It's all I want to ask you,' she promises. Her voice is growing thin and shrill, a gull's perhaps. 'It's all, really. Truly. What was it you were wanting to tell us, that day?'

The rocks are slippery enough to refuse her hysteria, and she slides back. She tries again, and when she arrives beside him she grapples confusedly with his clothing to hold herself steady.

'What was it?' she pleads, her fingers finally fluttering on his jacket. 'You were trying to tell us. But you never finished. Those students, they came and took you away. You wanted so much to tell us, but they didn't let you. What was it? Won't you say?'

Now he sees it may never be finished.

The eyes he has thought dull are bright and wild. The face he thought dour twitches and shines with appeal.

'It was the first time,' she explains, 'the first time I thought I was starting to understand anything, that day. And I thought I remembered things my father read me too, those bits of music far away. That's why you've got to tell me, you see.'

He tries to turn away, to shake free. But she clings. His limbs are weak, and for the moment he is voiceless. He is in his own worst nightmare.

The boy looks away. For a minute he has thought them likely to topple from the rocks, plunge into the sea; for one absurd second he thought they might be fighting. But the explanation is bound, he sees, to be simpler. His interest dwindles.

He pushes himself up, and wonders if he might swim today. It is the second day of his eighteenth year, yet may as well not have begun, for all the difference. He wonders whether anything can, or will.

'No,' he decides aloud. 'Nothing.' And stands bitter in the day.

'I wouldn't let it worry you, though,' says the cool and cheerful voice near him. 'Nothing is never as bad as it sounds. Or seems.'

He turns in panic to see the stranger who has come to sit quietly behind him, on the side of Hau hill. He is neither pleasant nor unpleasant in appearance, nor mocking. He is just sitting there, arms about his knees, with a faint smile.

'Nothing never is,' the man repeats.

He might have been some middle-aged gnome, to shoot up like that, from nowhere. His face is as lined as a lizard's. Or perhaps he is someone dreamed.

'How would you know?' the boy challenges. 'And who are you anyway?'

'One thing at a time,' this person says. 'I know about nothing because I've been alive the best part of fifty years. That's all. No other qualification to speak.' He is still smiling.

'So you know everything,' the boy says, 'because you've lived long enough. Is that it?'

'Not exactly. I make no claims.'

'All you people are the same.'

'What people?'

'You people my parents send along to talk to me. I thought they'd given up.'

'I don't know your parents.'

'That's a new one, then. Did they tell you to say that?'

'Hardly. Since I wouldn't know them if I saw them.'

'I'm supposed to believe that?'

'You don't have to believe anything. If you don't want to. I ought to warn you, though, that it never helps much. Sometimes you've got to accept that people mean what they say. Otherwise you're lost. These other people you talk about, what have they had to say?'

'The same as you. Cheer up, life's not so bad.'

'And that's all?'

'They always say they know I didn't mean it.'

'Mean what?'

'Mean to kill my sister, of course.'

'Oh,' the man says. He is no longer smiling.

'I suppose you're going to start on that now.'

The man is silent.

'Well, go on. Start. You might as well. Everyone else does.'

After a time the man shakes his head. 'No,' he says.

'You're not going to pretend you don't know about it. Everyone does. Everyone round here. If they just happen to be here a while, they're pretty soon told. I know by the way people steer clear. The only ones who come near are the people my parents send. Like you. That's how I know you. Anyone else would be scared off.'

The man appears very thoughtful. 'These others,' he asks, 'who have they been?'

'People who want to see if I'm right in the head. People who want to talk about what I should do with my life. And then there was that minister. He wasn't so bad.'

'Oh?'

'He only wanted to talk about God. I mean, not to me specially. Mostly to himself. He seemed to have some big problems.'

'I see.'

'So if you want my opinion, you're wasting your time. If I were you I wouldn't bother.'

'Fair enough. But there must be some things you'd like to talk about.'

'There must be,' the boy agrees. 'I can't think of any, though.' He starts to leave.

'And did you mean to?' the man calls after him.

The boy stops. He looks back with curiosity.

'Did you?' the man repeated. 'Did you really mean to kill your sister? That's what worries you more than anything, isn't it?'

'The first time anyone's asked me,' the boy says. He walks back, but looks out to sea. 'Really asked me. Funny when you think about it. Why haven't they?'

The man shrugs. 'It's an interesting point.'

'They all start off saying, of course we know you didn't mean to, but . . .'

'Naturally.'

'So who are you, then? What do they want this time?' He pauses. 'Usually they bring the people to the house. I get introduced to them. Are they trying something different this time?'

'You still haven't answered my question. Did you mean to?'

'That's easy,' the boy replies, hands behind his head, still looking out to sea. 'I don't know.' He hesitates. 'Sometimes I think yes. Sometimes I think no. I suppose that doesn't make sense to you.'

'It sounds very reasonable. And how did it happen?'

'It's no use you pretending you haven't been told I shot her. That's going too far. It's the first thing you'd be told.'

'But I haven't. I haven't been told anything.'

'Then I don't know what they're playing at this time. My parents, I mean. I might have known they had some new stunt. I wonder what it is?'

'I wouldn't know. I told you that. I told you I wouldn't even know what they looked like.'

'All right,' the boy says. 'Say I start trying to believe you.'

'That might be an idea.'

'You haven't even told me who you are.'

'Because you haven't given me a chance. I'm just someone who happens to be on this island. And sitting on this hillside. By pure chance, almost.'

'What does the almost mean?' Suspicious, the boy swings round.

'Nothing much. Just that I've seen you on this hill before. We both seem to like the view from up here, despite the climb. And perhaps because of the climb. We would have seen each other sooner or later, and probably spoken. So there's not too much chance in our meeting.'

'Why all the questions? If you really don't know me?'

'I didn't start them.'

'You've got a cheek.'

'I'm sorry, then. But you almost asked to be personal.'

'Mind your own business,' the boy replies, 'and go to hell.'

'I said I'm sorry.'

The boy laughs shortly. 'I bet. You can be too, if you like. Sorry for yourself. But don't be sorry for me. I've just about had a gutsful of that, lately.'

'I can guess,' the man says with sympathy.

'You couldn't. You couldn't guess. You couldn't know anything. So just shut up and quit spying.'

This time the boy leaves in earnest.

'Just one more thing,' the man calls after him. 'What is it you hate so much?'

'People,' the boy shouts back.

He stalks around a ridge and drops out of sight. The man lights a cigarette and finds his hands trembling. After a time, though, he allows his interest to be taken by the two figures on the rocks below. He wishes he could hear what they are saying.

Professor Thomson's voice is shaky. 'Remarkable,' he says. 'Quite remarkable.'

He holds up the object he has just scooped out of sea-wrack wedged in the rocks.

'Against all the rules, really,' he goes on. 'They're supposed to be very rare around here, and then only in deep water. This could even be the first to be found in this vicinity, for all I know. Perhaps that last storm brought it in.'

The girl kneels beside him. 'What is it?' she asks.

The dead creature in his hands is orange-red, fading patchily.

'A sea-star,' he says absently, turning it over.

'Yes, but—'

'A special one, of course,' he explains. 'A very special one.' He is almost tender.

'What makes it special?' The girl's face puckers with perplexity. 'It just looks like another sea-star to me.'

'If I'm right,' he says, 'and I hope I am, it's a member of the genus *plutonaster*. After Pluto, the god of the underworld. Because they live in perpetual dark on the floor of the ocean. Also called an abyssal star.'

The girl reaches out gently. 'And you're the first to find one here?'

'Probably. Of course one never knows how many have gone unseen. It's necessary to know what to look for.'

'And you do. So you found it here.'

She takes the star. It has a faint dead smell, but of the sea and not entirely unpleasant. 'It's nice to be able to know what to look for,' she adds in wonder. 'An abyssal star.' She pauses. 'I could have seen it and never known.'

'I imagine it will preserve. It's not too far gone.'

'I never know what to look for,' she goes on. 'I don't even know where to begin. That's why—'

'My best specimens, the fresh ones, I get from Yakich the fisherman,' he explains. 'The ones he finds in his nets. He puts them aside for me. I usually find only shallow-water species here. That's what makes this so special.'

He accepts the star from the girl's hands.

'That's why you've got to tell me,' she persists. 'It was the first time I thought I understood. Can't you see?'

'Of course this will be the prize specimen in my collection now. Naturally. But there are others almost as interesting too.'

'I've got to know what to look for,' she says. 'I've got to begin.'

He holds up the star. 'The longish arms and that unusually large sieve-plate are the distinguishing features,' he says. 'And the bright colour, of course. I'm afraid it will lose that colour when it's preserved, like most natural things. But still, the fact of the thing will be there. The substance.' He sighs. 'The shadow may elude us, but we can always lay our hands on the substance. Most reassuring.'

He smiles at the girl, for the first time. His day seems made.

'I can't hope for anything from Yakich while he's trying to entertain our friend the dolphin,' he adds. 'So this is rather an unexpected compensation, this star, out of the dark places of the sea. He couldn't have brought anything to match it. And besides, it wouldn't have been quite the same if he had found it. Still, it looks today as if his little affair with the dolphin might be over, wouldn't you agree? Sad, if so. We all seemed to enjoy the distraction, one way and another. We all goggled, like the children. And like children.'

He appears surprised and a little dismayed by his eloquence. Anyway he stops. And looks down at the sea rising near his feet.

'The tide,' he mutters. 'It won't wait for us to shift. We'd better go.' Perplexed, he looks at the girl, as if he has only just seen her there. 'I hope you've been interested. That at least you haven't been bored.'

'So you can't tell me,' she says, 'or won't.'

'But I've just . . .' He gestures helplessly with one hand, towards the star in the other. 'Tell you what?'

'What you said that day. So I can know what to look for.'

He moves back from the spitting sea. 'Surely you heard it was all a breakdown, just part of—'

'Of course. That's just what they would say. A breakdown.' She dismisses the word with contempt. 'It's what you said then that's important, not what they said after. Surely you can see. I really thought I started understanding. You hadn't had much interesting to say till that day. But it came so quick. If you could just—'

'I don't remember,' he says sharply.

He sees the dismay in her face.

'Because you don't want to?' she offers.

'All right,' he agrees, softening. 'There's that too.' There might be metal in his chest and throat, grating, cutting. 'There's that as well. But I still can't, still don't.'

'So now I know,' she says.

Her head is bent. He finds he has put a hand on her shoulder.

'You haven't told me your name,' he says.

'It's not important.'

'In one sense I expect it isn't. In another . . .' He shrugs. 'We name things so we can know them. People too. It helps.'

'And so we can forget them.'

'Sometimes,' he agrees.

'Zoe,' she answers. 'My name's Zoe. My father named me. My mother says it's too fancy for me. I should tell you I'm not supposed to be very bright. That was why I was taken from school when I was fifteen. The teachers said it was not much good me staying.' She raises her eyes briefly to his. 'They said I was difficult and took up too much of their time.' She looks down again.

'Well, Zoe,' he says, his hand still gentle on her shoulder, 'has it ever struck you that if you knew what to look for, you mightn't want to find it? Has it?'

Now kelp is flowing, tangling, in the risen tide. The mussel beds are sinking. Sea gargles into crevices on each side.

'Of course it has,' she replies. 'I often wonder if that's what happened to my father. That doesn't mean, though, I don't still want to know.' She shakes back her long hair, adjusts her old hat. Her gaze grows steady. 'But he used to say it was important to taste everything—taste everything real. The earth and trees, fruit and flowers, rain and sun, everything. To taste everything real to know anything.'

'Then . . .' He finds words difficult, for a moment.

'Yes?'

'Then he was probably right, of course,' he finishes. 'And we'd better go before we get wet feet, don't you think?'

'I'll take that, if you like,' she says, and reaches out for the star in his hands. 'I'll carry it back. I almost feel I found it too.'

His fingers do not resist when she plucks it away. She examines it again, more carefully. 'An abyssal star?' she says.

'That's the name,' he agrees.

'It's still just an ordinary star to me,' she says. 'But I suppose I could learn. I suppose the most surprising things are ordinary.'

She pushes an arm through his to help him over and off the sharp rocks, down to the pale level beach.

So there's an end to it [*he writes*]. My entry into the human world again and the botch I made of it. How much greater the comfort of the voyeur! I feel as exposed and vulnerable as ever I was. And hurt, as if I'd never suffered rejection before.

Yet when I retrace my steps—recall that conversation—it's hard to see how else it could have turned out. I was so taken aback, you see. It's one thing to anticipate a difficult adolescent, another to discover someone apparently regarded round here as a monstrous killer. I should have known—and if I hadn't imposed this monkish discretion upon myself, would have. Still, I must say it's been a help getting it all down. I don't suppose you expected to get another letter so soon, any more than I expected to write again so soon, and this really makes a mockery of my supposed solitude. It seems one must communicate, regardless. To live one must communicate, I mean. Even if one knows in advance it will all be misunderstood. Because I know you will. Misunderstand, I mean. You wouldn't believe I had any more than a reasonably human interest in the boy. And if I said fatherly you would laugh outright. Yet knowing me, living with me so long, surely doesn't entitle you to misunderstand, though it may entitle you to know more. Did I ever tell you I married? Of course I know perfectly well I haven't told you, because I don't believe I've told anyone in a dozen years. Often it seems it all happened to another person. We were both young, shiny with hope, and within the limits you know happy, for a while. We had a child. If happiness didn't last, it was as much her doing as mine. She resented the child, the change it brought, and me with it before long, perhaps because of my particular attachment to the child (someone had to offer it love, after all). It was precisely that restlessness of hers, which had so charmed me in the first place, which destroyed everything in the end. She walked out and I was left to bring up the boy. I think I managed surprisingly well, in retrospect. I don't mean I found it easy. It was demanding. The only real human demand I've known, in a way, and perhaps the most important one there is. Of course I wasn't a perfect father. I backslid often. I had to rely on other people to help out anyway. He was still at the napkin stage when she walked out on us and I couldn't manage him entirely by myself, expert though I may have been at changing napkins and warming bottles. Still, the fact is I created another human being; I created as surely as any artist. (And is there one work of art, anyway, which compares in richness and fascination and complexity with any single human being?) All ambition, everything I'd ever wanted, drained away into his life. My waking hours, whether I was actually with him or not, seemed to have only the one direction, and his demands didn't even cease when I slept—or tried to sleep. People, old acquaintances, claimed I was killing myself. They said I was a man obsessed. On top of that, they argued, I was evading myself, evading responsibility to myself and my own capabilities. Whatever that means, or meant; I'm not sure I know even now. (Couldn't they see there was one thing in my life I wanted to do well?) So far as I was concerned, I was capable as a father—and mother too—and only that counted. Naturally I took work where I could find it, but judged it less on its convenience and suitability for me than its convenience for him. It's true my physical condition wasn't the best, and this was what disturbed people. I often got run down. As illness became frequent, other things just seemed to get out of control: I couldn't cope. It was probably said, because I didn't want to cope; it was all doubtless psychosomatic. But that would have been as unfair and untrue as anything else that was said. When I packed the boy off to school for his first day—the cut lunch with fruit I'd carefully wrapped in his small schoolbag—I felt some relief. Other people were going to share the responsibility of bringing him up now. At the same time I felt a certain loss. I did, after all, fear falling back on myself, on my own shrunken resources. But neither feeling was to last. I was off work that day, having absented myself for the occasion, so I was at the door when he trailed home well ahead of time. He didn't like school, wasn't having any of it. A normal enough thing, of course. I had all the advice and reassurance in the world—from friends, from teachers. I sent him back to school the next day and he marched home again. I persisted, the next week and the next. He started refusing to go at all; I was powerless. I lost my job finally, because of absences, and had difficulty finding another. In the meantime I discovered the extent of my failure. As parent, mother and father all in one, I'd been so concerned with overcoming my obvious deficiencies that I hadn't observed I wasn't bringing my child up according to the comfortable norm. I really hadn't noticed. He was impatient with childish things, the rigmarole of the classroom. To regress in this way was beyond toleration. Moreover, he missed me. We'd been too close. We'd shared most things and he didn't see why I couldn't share school with him, and all its frustration. Or, failing that, why he shouldn't be with me most or all of the time. It was impossible, everything. My health cracked, and it seemed my mind might follow.

No, let me be honest or try to be. There is no understating it. My mind *did* follow. I managed survival on a diet of liquor and pills. I saw no one, went nowhere. Nor did I want to, it seemed. I was ready to shut up shop if I knew where the door was. Most of the time I wasn't even sure where the floor was.

At my lowest ebb, I sent a telegram to my ex-wife. (By this time we were legally divorced and I'd heard from a remote connection that she was married again and settled at last.) She arrived a couple of days later. I must say I hadn't expected much. I don't even remember quite what I wanted of her—other than sympathy, which was unlikely, and a little help. She flounced into our untidy flat aghast: how could we stand it? How did we manage to live like this? A few minutes later, in a quite casual way, she revealed that she now also had a child of her second marriage, and was apparently reconciled to it. She confessed she found it hard to believe she had ever taken our marriage seriously. It had all been a dreadful mistake, of course, and she hoped I didn't feel too badly about it. For herself, it had evidently been just part of some youthful phase. And she stepped back into the wreckage she had left in her wake—the flat, the boy, myself—with astonishment. I was too pathetically grateful to feel disgust, though I can now. It was obvious that if I hadn't sent my telegram she'd never have given us another thought. Yet in fairness I must say she was disturbed. After she'd given the flat a new look and bathed and dressed the boy decently, she sat down beside me with a sober expression and announced that one thing was obvious: I was inadequate, quite incapable of bringing up the boy. She should have guessed, she said. But never mind, things weren't hopeless. She could take the boy off my hands now. She would be quite happy to. In fact she saw no other solution. And nor—when I recovered from my shock—could I. She made the condition that I wasn't to intrude upon her second marriage, demand to see the boy, or otherwise make difficulty for her in bringing him up. I was stunned. Not to see my son at all? Was that what she meant? Yes, she said coolly, that was exactly what she meant. Couldn't I see that otherwise the job would be far too much for her? I sat silent, without will or strength to resist. My son, disturbed, crept into the room where we talked, sat on my knee and put his arms about my neck. It was even more impossible for me to think clearly. His trust was absolute, the most precious thing I'd ever earned and owned. I recall starting to weep, quite helpless. There were more tears, of course, before it all finished. I tried to bluff him into believing we should be together again before long. But he knew better. I had no more success in this than I'd had in persuading him to school. In the end I literally had to push him away at the railway station where we said goodbye. In his rage he began to kick at my shins, hit at me with his small fists. His mother tugged him off screaming; I saw her slap him several times before I turned away. It was all for the best: I had to believe that, or I could not survive. And survival was difficult enough anyway. I felt the new quiet and emptiness of the flat, when I got back there, like a pain. I groped my way from day to day, week to week, unable to forgive either my weakness or my betrayal. His stricken eyes haunted me, and the beat of those small fists upon my body. I tried, of course, to keep in touch. But my ex-wife never wrote. And the money and presents I tried to send the boy were returned without comment. After a while the post office took upon itself the duty of returning my attempts at communication. I lost touch altogether. I couldn't even imagine his environment: so long as I had an address I could let my fancy work. Still, there is compensation in an atrophied imagination, as there is in an atrophied conscience. I had both, for what they were worth. It meant I could engage without hope of commitment in what I had left of life. And take it lightly. As I did, and as you know

I have, better than anyone. I slid back among people for whom my marriage and child had always been a joke. Besides, I couldn't stand anyone who might have sympathy. Now I see myself in the mirror, a middle-aged pansy, adrift. Could I have been anything more? I daren't answer that question, much as I can be ruthless about that face in the mirror. Is there anything else to tell? Only that for years I held to the faint hope that my son would eventually, inevitably, find his way back to me. Was that so absurd? The blow need never have fallen—I need never have been woken from this dream—but life has a cruel way of gloating. The week before I came over here I met in the street a friend of my wife's I hadn't seen in fifteen years or more. A fascinated victim, eager to place my head upon the execution block, I asked if she'd had sight of my child, my son, in recent years. Well, not really, she said. Only that once, at the funeral. The funeral? Of course. Jenny's—my ex-wife's—funeral. She had gone down to it, but had to leave straight after. She hadn't seen much of Jenny in her last years, because they'd fallen out. She hadn't even heard of Jenny's illness until just before her death. She would have visited Jenny in hospital but the death came so suddenly. But surely I knew? Time went so fast, it must have been all of two years now. But my boy, I remembered to ask, my son? She remembered him at the funeral, that was all. The eldest and tallest of Jenny's four sons. They'd all been there. She remembered him as a pleasant, extremely good-looking young man with his hand on his stepfather's arm. And thoughtful. He led his stepfather away from the graveside and shook hands with most of the mourners himself, to save his stepfather. So gently spoken. He impressed her, though they exchanged only a few words. She supposed he must be nearly through university now. Well, if I'd just excuse her, it was one of her few trips to town, and she had so much . . .

She must have seen my face, and been afraid. After all, it wasn't her problem. She scurried out of my life again, a plump elderly woman with a shopping basket. Who might just have thrown a fist in my stomach, a grenade in my face.

If you thought me strange, those last few days, there is a reason. The strangeness wasn't altogether because I was contemplating escape to this place. Nor was it entirely because of your recent behaviour.

Is life tolerable entirely without hope? Anyway it's an interesting experiment, new to me.

Oh yes, and that dolphin didn't come back today.

Very best wishes,

Tony

He begins deleting, one line and then another. The deletions smudge, merge. In the end he just shreds the pages one by one. He wonders if another trip to the beach might be worthwhile.

ELEVEN

Frank Yakich is off in town, or home mending his nets. You can take your pick of the stories. Or he may still be reading about himself in the newspaper. There has been a single-column picture of Frank, and a half dozen short paragraphs headed *Fishy Visitor to Holiday Beach*. Anyway he doesn't go out in his launch.

The truth is that Frank's wife is off colour, and fishing is never up to much at this time of month. And he feels he has earned a day off, with all the excitement, now almost gone from the beach.

The reporter rings Harry Green again at the Bella Vista. The idiot doesn't seem to realize that the place is no longer in business, and Harry thus no longer a public person. 'Nothing doing,' Harry nevertheless says helpfully. 'It's all over. We're back to normal. I wouldn't waste the boss's money on these toll calls again if I were you.'

He replaces the receiver. 'No news is good news,' he observes to his wife. 'No doubt about that.'

Yet he goes outside, after, and looks at the sea, as if he can no longer trust it. Nondescript individuals are walking the beach, perhaps only a few more than usual. And there is no more than an average number of swimmers, for this time of year.

Frank Yakich too is watching the sea, nursing a large glass of his own red wine in one hand while he shades his eyes with the other. The sky is patchy with cloud, and the sea freaked with shadow. And a distant fragment of mainland, usually sharp and blue, is faint and hazy.

Still a characterless day, one which may never find itself.

Jean wakes late and decides against breakfast, because of her stomach. Sleeping-pills have seen her through the night, but leave her dull and queasy. There is also an inexplicable ache in her temple. The third night, the third day. Absurd to think he might return now, and futile. The inside of the shack, once tight, has grown vastly empty. Almost echoing. She is back in an existence where perhaps only pills offer comfort. It isn't strange to her. She can remember just one other comfort so real; speed. But there was an end to that consolation. After one disappointment she hurled a car along a highway until tyres gave, brakes too, and the vehicle screamed into somersaults. She was not much damaged, though the car was a wreck. Nevertheless she found all she might find in that direction. If she drives at more modest pace now it is not because she is afraid, but because she isn't.

She swings abruptly to the floor, with a slap of feet. And walks the floor naked, back and forward, as if engaged in some search. Her body remains large and heavy, her mind dazed with sleep. The space around her seems to expand, the walls of the shack to recede. The ache in her temple persists, though she appears to think she might prise it out with pressing fingertips. Incredible that she has ever seen death, the fear or idea of death, as a test. Survival is the only real test, survival. True, its failures are hidden beneath euphemism. But the fact remains; and the act.

She has known that for some time, though she has also tried to ignore it. She can learn to sleep with it again, in place of Ted. If it grows more difficult with time, that is surely part of the test too.

In the meantime she can slip into her bathing costume, shut the door of the shack and walk down to the sea, still with hope of awakening. She accepts the acrid smell of manuka and dying lupins, the cool clay and then sliding sand beneath her feet, the querulous sky above. She feels apathy drain from her body as she nears the sea. Eager for sensation now, she wades into the water, until it rises above her thighs, and then dives. The water is sharp and cleansing. She swims underwater some way and finally surfaces gasping, shaking her head. It is late in the morning and there are few other swimmers visible about the south end of the beach: just a head or floating figure here and there. Hau hill stands dark and craggy against the clouds; Hau headland is a cold arm embracing the bay. She swims further out, until there is only one bobbing head in near view. Then she recognizes the face: the neatly casual man alone on the beach. A rather tired swimmer, lumbering and methodical, evidently determined to make a business of it. But not totally inadequate in this element. She spins down deep into the green water, rises again. He is almost stationary now, treading water. He appears intent on something, then he cries out.

She rolls in the water, shifting her gaze just in time to see the flash of fin, the turbulence behind. For an instant she is flimsy with fright. Her heart is huge, her mouth dry.

Then she remembers.

And the creature rises again, nearer, water falling white from its dark body. With a twitch of its comic nose and a flick of tail, it leaps. Jean rocks in the violent water as the dolphin crashes down and swirls past her. She could almost have touched. She is laughing now, with relief.

Her laughter has echo. She swings her head and sees the convulsed man. The dolphin is streaking toward him, half out of the water, and then around. Before Jean can get her breath it is heading back to her again. It seems to fly rather than swim, to glide upon scattering skeins of foam.

The man waves. In delight, it seems, as the dolphin weaves between and around them, repeating a figure eight. They might, the three of them, be partners in some elaborate dance. But all so fast, there is never time to breathe, for anything other than laughter. She waves back to the man, but without voice to call. They seem to be nearer, and perhaps are, as the dolphin tightens its loops.

Once she thinks she feels it as it brushes past; and tries to tell the man.

The dolphin slows, stops, sways at a distance. The man swims awkwardly to her.

'My God,' she says. 'I still can't believe it.'

'Then you'd better start,' he observes dryly. 'Someone has to.'

For now the dolphin is circling slowly.

'And since we're here,' he goes on, 'the real problem is not believing it, but how we make friends.'

'I wouldn't have thought that the problem.'

'True. But it's all a little one-sided, wouldn't you say?' He treads water beside her as she tries to recover her breath. 'We ought to show some response. Otherwise . . .'

'Yes?' she says. 'Otherwise?'

'Well, otherwise it might lose interest. That's obvious.'

'I wouldn't know. Never having been befriended by a dolphin before.'

'The principle,' he says, 'has fairly general application.'

'What kind of response, then?'

'Now you have me. Since we haven't got bells and trumpets, we might try splashing about a bit. To show we know it's there. Or to show we're here. Hail, stranger, we come in peace – that kind of thing. It might also see we're not altogether devoid of vitality.'

'I think it touched me,' she remembers. 'Almost. As it went past. Sorry if I'm slow. It's still so unreal, about the last thing I can cope with this morning. I just can't—'

'Try,' he says. 'Think of the how, not the why. All right?'

'All right. Whatever you say.'

She smiles. There is still something of a vanquished urchin in his face. Something of an excited boy trapped in a weary wisecracker. Yet he isn't altogether grotesque.

'You splash that way,' he says, 'I'll splash this. If it comes close enough, you might try to touch it gently. In an affectionate way. It might respond.'

'Do you think I might leap on its back?' she asks, trying to keep a straight face.

'Not at the beginning,' he says seriously. 'First things first.'

It is too much for her. She giggles. Now, she thinks, who is the child?

He floats on his back, splashing with his hands and kicking. Jean, after hesitation, does the same. With her head to one side she watches the dolphin. It reacts immediately. First away, then back in a wide sweep.

'Now stop,' the man says. 'Let it look.'

They drift alongside each other. The dolphin cruises around.

'Still unsure,' the man says. 'At least we've got him interested.'

'It might be a her,' Jean observes lightly.

'Him or her, then. Or it.'

Their bodies bump gently, with the pull of the tide. Jean feels faintly absurd, waiting on the dolphin. Disposed so passively, she could be waiting on something much more predictable.

'We'll splash in turn,' he says. 'First you, then me. Then perhaps together. Give him a little variety.'

Jean, again on the point of giggling, and perhaps hiccups, thrashes about on the water. She stops and the man starts. The dolphin swims from side to side, faster and faster, like someone pacing back and forward in impatience. Still at a distance, though. She joins the man in splashing and the dolphin, dark back gleaming, noses forward slowly.

'We're winning,' he gasps. 'It's coming.'

Then, incredibly, it strikes.

It speeds forward, half risen from the water, its impetus tossing them apart. They are everywhere and nowhere. Jean swallows salt and rises choking. Just in time to see the dolphin wheel, flick, and crash between them again. And again she is all arms and legs, her companion still lost somewhere in the dazing water. Now she feels panic in her throat. The third time, she feels the dolphin beyond all doubt, in sliding impact across her stomach. Yet the touch is so swift her flesh can recall nothing but the alien sensation, nothing of the actual substance. She tries to swim clear of the melee, but she has lost sense of direction, the dolphin seems all around, swerving, flicking, leaping, with the water wild. And there seems no possible end, except one, for she surely cannot last. She is swallowing more sea. The bruising water starts to cling, to drag, and her limbs are helpless. She only needs to stop struggling, for relief. It has to stop, has to. Once more she is buffeted lightly by the creature. The dark flesh heaves across her vision. In terror she strikes out blind and crashes against something. Not the dolphin, but the man. He is still there, safe, and takes her shoulders. And it appears to be all over.

It is all over. The dolphin rests on the surface three or four yards away, nose upthrust as if in query, slightly palpitating and perhaps exhausted.

'My God,' is all Jean can say, dizzy.

'We can't complain that it didn't respond,' the man declares. 'At least.'

'Respond?' Jean tries to gather herself. 'Not for me, thanks. I wouldn't care if it never responded again.'

'We may have been a little too vigorous ourselves, trying to attract it. It may just have reacted in kind.'

'You're too sweet and reasonable. You think that thing is?'

'I'm only suggesting we may have misled it. About our capacity for sport in the water, I mean.'

'You call that sport? That?'

'Well . . .'

'All I want to know is how to get away from it.'

But her panic ebbs. She has survived, after all, still improbably intact.

'A minute ago you were keen to leap on its back,' he recalls. 'Or perhaps I didn't hear right.'

'Pure optimism,' she says, 'in the glow of ignorance. I've lost all ambition.'

'It appears to be waiting on us again.'

'Let it wait.'

'Actually it was quite careful.'

'Careful? Perhaps it's me who's not hearing right.'

'Notice how it avoided crashing into us directly. It could have. I'd say it was a matter of accurate timing for a creature that size at full speed. It wasn't being more than playful.'

'How naive can you be? That thing's wild.'

'Also intelligent,' he observes, 'according to all I've read. Perhaps next to us the most intelligent of living things.'

'I'm profoundly unimpressed. I can remember dangerous drunks with a pretty high I.Q. I tell you it's wild.'

'True,' he agrees. 'But surely that makes it more interesting.'

The dolphin is swimming back and forward again, apparently waiting. It is between them and the shore.

'Well,' she says, 'what now? Incidentally, I don't even know your name.'

'Adams; Tony Adams. Short and forgettable, a great advantage.' He nods toward the dolphin. 'I suggest we take things calmly. Swim back to shore with as little disturbance of the water as possible. In view of the way you feel, I mean. Of course it might just follow. But—'

'You haven't asked mine,' she says.

'Yours?' He looks puzzled.

'My name.'

'Of course. Sorry. Just too preoccupied. Besides, it's hardly the place . . .'

'Jean well, Jean Anyone. Never mind.'

'I've seen you round. I almost felt I knew you anyway. I suggest we try swimming past it, one each side. How's that suit you? Game?' He pauses. 'You're alone here?'

'I had a friend. He's gone.'

'I see.'

'I'm not particularly bereft, if that's what you see.'

'I didn't mean that. I didn't mean anything. Your business. Each side, then? Let's take it quietly.'

They swim, and part. Jean moves through the water with restrained effort, a flutter of fear in her stomach, ten to fifteen yards wide of the dolphin.

The dolphin tosses its head this way and that, with quizzical tilt, trying to make up its mind. In a few moments they are in a precise line, the three of them, the dolphin exactly at the centre. The dolphin swings and dips gracefully, then rises and falls as it swims slowly between them, with them, toward the shore.

The man, Tony, is right. It will respond in kind, has. It is still difficult to believe, though. Too much, for one morning. And they are actually taking it inshore, or is it taking them? Now it is just a little ahead, and they swim in V formation.

'See?' Tony calls in satisfaction, pausing. 'We can take it back for the kids to see.'

Then, with slight tremor of its body, the creature, perhaps grown impatient, speeds ahead and arcs back to them. Jean and the man look at each other perplexed. It seems to have vanished without a ripple.

'Start swimming again,' Tony shouts. 'Probably just clowning.'

She does as he suggests, but convinced it is gone. The loss seems personal. He is swimming again too, but fitfully, stopping to look back over his shoulder for the fin. Their directions appear to be converging, without the dolphin between, anyway the gap is closing. Too sad, she thinks, if they lose the creature now.

The tap, on one leg and then the other, is light and quite tentative. Perhaps she cries out. Certainly her flesh does. Then the tip of something, nose or tail, brushes across her stomach.

Her throat trembles, but she finds her voice. 'It's swimming underneath me,' she calls. 'Underneath. Tony, you hear?'

I must be all but riding on it, she thinks. All but.

Exhilarated, she lets herself sink a little, toward the back of the creature, and then feels cheated when it surfaces just ahead with spouting blowhole. I ought to grab its tail, she thinks gaily, hitch a lift. But Tony may be right, first things first. Anyway now she is swimming alongside the dolphin. It rolls and dips almost in parody of her motion as it swims beside her, never getting ahead. At times it is less than a yard away, seldom much more. Already they are quite close to the beach, into shallower water.

'Taken a fancy to you,' Tony says, swimming up on her free side. 'Must be male after all.'

'Doesn't mean a thing,' she replies breathless. 'We women often stick together.'

'Think you can take it in much further?' he gasps. 'Look at the crowd up there.'

It is remarkable. The dark clot of onlookers on the pale shore is thickening by the minute. There must be already two or three hundred people watching, almost the entire population of the bay. And there are stragglers, hurrying, hobbling. And children darting.

'I assume it has a mind of its own,' Jean says. 'If it wants to come with me, it will.'

They put their heads down again. The dolphin stays with them, only now and then nosing ahead. When they look up the crowd seems twice as large. Certainly it is closer. And breaking up into individual parts. The skittering children, the motionless aged. Men and women rolling up trousers or pulling up skirts to enter the water for a closer look. Others stripped to bathing-costume, knee-deep and waiting. Tony and Jean become aware of the noise, the separate shouts merging in one reverberant cry, as if from a single being.

They may, Tony thinks, ruin everything, scare it away. That would be the finish, perhaps for good. Before the kids even have a chance. He tries to lift himself higher from the water, to gesture them clear. He also shouts for them to keep back. No one hears. No one wants to hear. He is a side issue, even more so than Jean.

All that happens, in fact, is that Jean and the dolphin get ahead of him. So that he is more ineffectual than ever.

To hell with them, then. He doesn't want to be conquering hero anyway. He drops even further behind.

But the kids, he remembers, too late.

Professor Thomson walks freely this morning, unburdened, easy for the first time in a week. Until the crowd on the beach blocks his way and he sees what they see. Two bathers in the middle distance, and a dolphin. The dolphin.

He is, for a time, as transfixed as anyone else. Then the desire for speech grows stronger, stronger than he has known it for a year. He grows aware of the girl who has appeared at his elbow, and this time is not dismayed by her appearance. It is as if his need has called her up. And in a sense, though he disputes the knowledge, he knows this true; she is as much creation of his need as she was, evidently, of her father's. Does that imply responsibility? Perhaps. If only. If only he had something to say. To tell.

But there is the dolphin.

'They are supposed to be drowned sailors,' he informs her. 'In the Greek legend. Changed by the god Dionysus. Thereafter they stood for kindness and virtue in the sea.'

The girl says nothing, but places her arm through his in the same shy manner as she did the day before.

'Like all legends,' he goes on, 'it has a seed of truth. They are mammals which once, in different form, lived on the land, like us. For some reason, though, they chose the sea as home. Why?' He shrugs. 'They have lungs, as we have. They are warm blooded, as we are. Their young are babies which need their mother's milk, like ours. And they are sometimes supposed to be the most intelligent of creatures, along with man. So why should they have chosen the sea?'

The girl stirs beside him. Now she has taken faint grip on his arm, as if to reassure. 'Perhaps,' she observes, 'there wasn't room for them— and us too.'

'Perhaps,' he agrees. 'Though I doubt evolution would support the argument. Still, even if we weren't here when they made the choice, they might have seen us coming. Or something very like us. And made the choice in anticipation. They might at least have been confident they would have the sea to themselves, unlike the land. Intelligence would give them advantage. When we, or something like us, were only beginning to rise upright.'

The bathers, a man and a woman, are swimming closer inshore with the dolphin.

'They hid away from us,' she insists, 'in the water. That's what I mean. Because they wouldn't have stood for us. Or we for them.'

'Not quite,' he says. 'Otherwise how explain the stories of man and dolphin which survive from pagan times? As legends, true. But there must have been some original truth as substance. There was Odysseus. A dolphin saved the life of his son, Telemachos, when the child fell into deep water. The dolphin came to the boy's aid and swam with him back to the beach. And then there was Arion, the most beautiful of singers in Greece. Herodotos wrote down his story, two hundred years after. He told how Arion was cast into the sea by piratical Corinthians, but was saved by a dolphin who carried the singer on his back.'

'They haven't had much to do with us since, though, have they?' the girl says. 'Unless we trap them, like we trap everything, and make them sing for their supper.'

'True.'

'I wonder why. Don't you? Don't you wonder why?' She pauses. 'I do. And I wonder why this one . . .'

She hesitates, and her grip tightens.

'Yes?' he says. 'This one?' It is still nearer the shore, with the swimmers, and the excitement around grows. 'This one?' he repeats, hardly able to hear himself.

'Perhaps it thinks we might be ready again. We, all of us.' Her voice just carries to him, above the noise. 'Don't you think it might?'

He bends toward her. She might be looking at the dolphin and the swimmers, or even further. Her eyes have a slight glaze and a certain calm. 'To be fanciful,' he agrees, 'yes.'

'But I'm not,' she says, and he has no reason to disbelieve her. 'It might just be that we're ready again.'

'And it might just be,' he argues, 'that this one doesn't know us.' He is still bent toward her. And he speaks, to his surprise, with the intensity her expression appears to demand. 'To be equally fanciful,' he goes on, 'it might just be that we're new here, on this shore. Our kind. So new. You might consider that too. The Maoris had their stories of taniwha, sea creatures sometimes specially kind to man, legends rather like those of the Greeks. And after all they were pagan too. I mean just that they sought revelation in earth and sea and forest and sky and rock and river, and in all things, in all they could see and name and learn to know. Not in abstraction. When we gave ourselves to abstraction we gave this world away. What greater betrayal could there have been? Surely the world, all things, must have felt it. When we placed ourselves above. For we had to make the abstraction in our image. Naturally. Nothing else would have been good enough, other than that we worship ourselves. And in time learn to hate ourselves too.'

He takes breath. He has begun to think he might not stop. And it is after all only flesh which drags him back. He seems to have been plunging through abandoned rooms, one after the other, faster and faster, and then into still emptier places. He is not even sure, now, where he has found himself, or how.

She is tugging at his arm. 'Go on,' she pleads. 'Go on.'

The day and the place close around him again: the day, the beach, the crowd, the noise reaching new peak. Like his flesh, an inescapable garment. Inescapable and shrinkable and impossibly tight. For something strangles.

'I—' he begins.

'Quickly,' she says. 'Go on.'

'I told you,' he protests. 'I told you we were being fanciful.'

'No,' she insists. 'No.'

And she tugs at his arm again, as if she might cause more words to tumble.

'Please,' he says, and shakes his head.

'You're afraid.'

'That's one way of putting it.' But his reply is lost in the uproar. The swimmers have at last brought the dolphin within a few yards of shore, into water so shallow and clear that onlookers can see its entire shape, even its gently moving tail. Then the first wave of people go into the sea after it. The water explodes. For a moment it is impossible to see what is happening. Children squeal and scream in panic. An old man on crutches is knocked sideways and ignored. A man perhaps already shaky with liquor falls or plunges into the sea fully dressed, and his jacket floats up under his armpits. A woman has hysteria.

'Golphin, golphin,' comes a clear, shrill child's cry. 'Want to see golphin.'

Under frantic feet the sand churns, the water sprays. Then people see it, or most do. The dolphin rises shining and seems actually to stand on its tail for an instant, swivelling. And then diving, almost noiselessly, and speeding away into less confined water. Soon they can barely see its fin out in the bay. A child is weeping.

The hand on his arm has gone limp. It has all happened very quickly. He becomes aware that a fine rain is falling, and apparently has been for some time. They turn together, and on impulse he places a hand over hers, consoling. Most people around are as stunned and silent as they. Already there is bumping, shuffling, oddly quiet retreat from the sea. Only the children can be heard clearly, against the dull mutters of the old. And then even they are quiet. 'Well,' he says. 'So they, we, lost it.'

'It must have found it was wrong,' she says steadily. 'We weren't ready after all.'

'Or too ready,' he amends.

'Or too ready,' she accepts, after a time, as they walk together along the shore.

The crowd has almost dispersed altogether when they leave the water. 'Well,' Tony says, 'we tried.' He bends to recover his trodden towel. 'Pity about the kids, though.'

'The kids?'

'About them having no chance. They were lost in the stampede.'

'I expect they were. So were we.'

'If the kids had been given a quiet chance, perhaps it wouldn't have turned tail.'

Jean shrugs. 'I almost turned tail myself,' she observes. 'Still, I won't say I didn't enjoy it all. Even the sudden end. What more did you expect, or what else?'

Tony hesitates. 'Never mind,' he replies finally. 'I'm just saying it was too bad about the kids, that's all.'

'I heard you the first time.'

'Then forget it.' He is tired and, denied climax, disappointed. Everything has fizzled out: he is left with a rainy beach, scattering people, a woman he does not know and may not care to know. 'Still unreal?' he asks.

'Give me a night to sleep on it.'

'You're welcome.'

The rain is thickening. He decides it futile to attempt drying himself and throws the towel over his shoulder. Chilled, he looks among the retreating figures for someone who might resemble the Garland boy. Is that it, then, is that why he happens to have come to the beach on so uninviting a morning? In expectation of seeing the boy again? Yet he hopes not. He hopes to Christ not. He does not care, on the whole, to inspect his feeling about the boy. For, whatever the feeling is exactly, it is bound not to bear painless inspection. If looking for the boy anyway, he has found the dolphin. And Jean, of course. No forgetting her.

'A drink or two would warm us,' she observes.

'True. Shall we take off to the pub, then?'

'Not to the pub. To my place.'

'Your place, then. If that's all right.'

'Why shouldn't it be?' she asks, rather aggressively.

His diffidence appears to have undone him again. 'It's just,' he blunders on, 'just I don't want to intrude. You needn't feel obliged.'

'Obliged?' she laughs. 'I wouldn't know the meaning of the word.'

Too forced a front, he decides; he sees her as bluffly pathetic. As he walks off with her, he looks back once to the beach. It is quite deserted under the rain. And the rain is beginning to obscure the hills and headlands of the island. There really isn't anyone to be seen.

'Now I think about it,' Jean says, 'it really was quite wonderful, while it lasted.'

'Something out of a storybook?' he offers.

'I suppose that's what I mean. Yes.' She turns and smiles vaguely as they walk the clay track between the tall manuka. 'Pinch me and say we all lived happily ever after.'

Ben Blackwood ambles home, his clothes sopping, his spectacles misted. He was possibly the last person in the bay to heed the calls from the beach; and he is, almost certainly, the last to leave. In the haze of his indifferent vision everyone seems to disappear quite magically, and he is dawdling across the sand alone. His clothes grow heavy with moisture, but he feels no weight. On his way home he purchases smoked oysters from the store. He often buys them for himself as bribe or reward, as a treat for supper, when he is working well, or expecting to work well. He once had almost certainly ill-founded belief in their aphrodisiac potential, and even now clings faintly to the idea that they may also offer some more cerebral stimulation. When he gets home, though, he does no more than sit damp at his desk. He sits there perhaps an hour. After a while, unbribed, he eats the smoked oysters for lunch.

TWELVE

It is early, just after sunrise, when Tony knocks on the door of Jean's shack. 'Ready?' he calls.

She comes to the door holding a dressing-gown about her body. Her eyes are hazy and plainly difficult to focus. More than a hangover, he decides. She is quite stupid with drugs.

'Ready?' he repeats.

'Oh,' she says vaguely. 'Yes.' But she still hesitates. She starts to come toward him, then backs away.

'For that swim,' he explains. 'That search we planned this morning. Remember?'

'Of course.' Heavy and confused, she hesitates again. 'In just a minute. I'll be ready in just a minute. That's all. I just have to get into my swim-suit.'

They arranged this meeting last night. It was his proposal to look for the dolphin before other people were about. He lights a cigarette while waiting for Jean to emerge from the shack. But his mouth is too dry to enjoy it and he tosses it away half-smoked. The bay is pleasantly warm and still in the early light. Despite the woman, his expectations are still sharp: he seems to have surprised the morning, and himself.

She arrives beside him, still dull and confused, and together they walk in silence down through the manuka to the sea. The beach is perfectly empty. The morning would be hard to better. And they have it absolutely to themselves: the hills and headlands, sand and sea, tipped and tinged with lemon light. He feels the sun gentle on his skin as he walks into the water, the woman a little way behind. The sea too seems to have the flawless flavour of morning as it rustles cool about him. He launches himself, travels underwater a few yards, surfaces and kicks out. After a while he twists round to see if the woman is following. She swims with what appears desperate concentration, seldom lifting her head. When she nears him she offers a faint, tight smile, her first. She seems to know who he is, now the water has woken her.

They are possibly two hundred yards out from shore when the fin rises ahead.

The dolphin approaches him first, though it remains out of reach as it circles. He is sure that the creature knows him; he treads water patiently, waiting upon it to come still closer. He feels certain it will, this morning. Then to his dismay Jean begins splashing, with vigour and perhaps irritation, and the dolphin swings abruptly towards her. Again circling, but this time the circles shrink. Until, yes, he is certain they have touched, and touched again. Jean dips under the water entirely, apparently moving with the dolphin. The water is too disturbed for him to see. Then with a shimmer of sea and light they rise together, pale woman and dark dolphin, Jean's arms lightly about the clown's head. They part in almost the same instant, swerving in different directions and yet coming together again, spinning, swaying, and at last swimming together. Their understanding appears perfect.

He may as well face it: he has become superfluous. He watches them move away in frolic. The woman seems to glow in the water as she abandons herself with the creature. He swims around them, at discreet distance, but neither appears interested in his presence. Finally he floats on his back, drifting, waiting till their game is done.

After a while he looks back to shore. No crowd there today: no one has yet seen. The untrodden beach shines above the flickering waterline. But then, yes, there is someone. At the south end of the beach, near the rocks, a single figure.

So it is only a matter of minutes, now, before the whole of Te Hianinu Bay is roused for the new day's sensation. He supposes he and Jean have had their fun anyway. Certainly she has. He just hopes the kids have a chance today.

Then he looks again at the single figure on the shore, this time with twinge of recognition, and knows the rousing of the bay unlikely.

He swims inshore to talk. The boy is just in the act of entering the water. Tony wades to meet him. 'You see it?' he says.

He points unnecessarily. The woman and romping dolphin are, after all, quite visible.

'I'm not blind,' says the boy.

'We have it tame,' Tony continues, as if arguing a cause. 'We've had it out there twenty minutes.'

'Marvellous.'

'You're not interested?'

The boy doesn't reply. He continues into the water.

'For God's sake,' Tony says.

The boy looks back in cool query.

'If that, out there, doesn't interest you, what does?' Tony asks. 'You're not likely to see anything like it again in your life, are you?' He receives no answer.

'Yesterday,' he persists, 'I tried to bring it in for the kids. For the same reason, something once in their lifetime. And because they'd have loved it. But the crowd scared it off. I even thought you might be interested in giving me a hand today. What's the matter with you?'

The boy shrugs. But remains, nevertheless.

'You can't be bitter about a dolphin, for God's sake. You can't hate everything. It's not going to bring your sister back to life, is it now?'

'How would you know?' the boy demands.

But the boy has lingered long enough for Tony to feel some victory near, perhaps.

'It's obvious,' Tony replies lamely.

'Then you don't know anything,' the boy announces. 'Go to hell.'

He casts himself forward, diving deep, and eventually swims out into the bay at an angle which will take him well clear of Jean and the dolphin. For the second time that short morning Tony sees something escape him; he feels not only superfluous but unreal, attempting a failing, phantom grip on the world.

He grits his teeth and swims. He batters the water rather than propels himself through it. But the indifferent sea wins, of course. Soon his body aches. The punishment is his. And his effort is smothered in his wake. His lungs hurt too, for he can cheat himself of only so much air. He lifts his head briefly, long enough to feel the nip of new air in his chest, and continues striking out. Even his early mornings, which he has had to himself so long, seem gone. If this one is to be typical:

that inquisitive fool on the beach, the woman and the dolphin out in the water. They are taking over. And soon a crowd will grow, just as one has with every appearance of the damn fish. He wishes it a shark again.

What does that fool know about hate? Hate? He sees it as solid now, sure and solid, the only thing he can trust. For within its wall he is safe from himself. Safe from people; safe from fools. And safe with what he cannot forget.

He swims, about twenty yards out from the rocks, parallel to Hau headland. When he is well out from the beach, near a quarter-mile, he allows himself a quick look back. The woman is between himself and the beach, still involved with the dolphin, and the man is swimming out to join them. Still no one about on the beach. He really has no cause for complaint. After all the other three occupy only a microscopic portion of his own Pacific. He has the rest to himself, if he likes. He begins swimming, in more considered fashion, towards the tip of the headland. He doesn't look back again. —

As he falls into the rhythm of swimming, his anger decreases. His limbs join gentler discourse with the water. It can soothe, if not heal. And its response is predictable, though he likes it on rougher days, with tossing swell. Now he seems just skimming across its surface. He may feel at home here on occasion, as nowhere else, but in the end is never deceived; it is only the distance, no more. And always a cheat, for he has to return. To his parents, their faces; to people, their silence. To the empty place where Diana has been. Can that never fill, ever? Can it anyway, ever? He has no way of knowing. His own experience tells nothing, and he cannot imagine anything which may. He overhears his parents tell each other, like a prayer, that it is just a question of waiting. Who, he or them? And what for? Then the old questions fall away from him, shed leaves, and he is lulled mindless in his own motion.

Until, that is, the sea surprisingly seethes beside him. The dolphin kicks out of the water, leaping high, and he is tossed in its turbulence. Then it is bouncing ahead, behind, all around. Dazed, he gropes for a direction, but finds none. It seems the sea may never cease to erupt.

But it calms eventually. The dolphin swims close and perhaps intentionally nudges him; he cannot decide one way or the other, though the creature is evidently not repelled by their contact. He looks back toward the shore, at the man and woman watching. They are stationary in the water. He is tempted to call that they can have the damn thing back, and welcome. Instead he makes the same point clear by striking out directly for the beach.

The dolphin rises and falls beside him, quite perversely. He changes direction, and so does it. There is no escape that way. He dives and it dives beside him. They surface together. If he goes fast, it does. If he slows, it slows. It might be tied to him. Or a shadow.

'Get out,' he shouts, and lashes out with a foot in despair. But his foot strikes glancingly off the side of the dolphin, and it twitches its tail wilfully in return. Or perhaps just amiably; he is too angry to care.

He is near the other two swimmers now, at least within forty yards. They are still watching, with their absurd smiles.

He decides to ignore it altogether. It really presents no impediment, now, to his return to shore. It is just irritating, that is all. He swims with steady stroke toward the beach, lifting his head only to breathe. Until he collides with the dolphin, or the dolphin with him. Anyhow there it is, blocking his way. He tries to duck beneath it, and the dolphin ducks too. He becomes involved with its flippers and suede body as he rises, fighting himself clear. He cannot make up his mind if it has just lurched against him or if he has deliberately been pushed toward open sea again. Its head shoots up, the long snout inches from his face, with a sleepy smile. A sleepy smile which never changes; a frightening parody of a smile. He starts to push it clear, tries to heave it away. But it is a dead weight. No matter how he struggles he cannot seem to shift it an inch. Finally he collapses against its flank, his arms limp about its neck, and rests there supported by the buoyancy of the dolphin. It makes no objection to his weight. It remains perfectly still as he gets his breath, recovers his strength. After a while he recognizes that he has given in. He begins to laugh feebly, rustily. Anyway the sound surprises him.

The sun is strong now. Tony and Jean wade out of the water. Then they look back at the boy. He still floats with the dolphin.

'We ought to have known,' Tony says.

'Known what?' Jean looks irritable.

'About the boy. It seems there always has to be a boy.'

'What are you talking about?'

'A boy and a dolphin,' he explains. 'All the stories. It seems there must be something to them.'

Now they are swimming together, the dolphin and the boy, no more than inches apart, so close they might be the one queer beast.

'We can't compete,' Tony adds. 'That's all I'm saying.'

They are circling. Then Tony sees the boy has stopped swimming. The dolphin now appears to be towing him along.

'Speak for yourself,' Jean says. 'I think I did fairly well. Anyway, who tamed it?'

'We may have; and the fisherman. True. But it appears to have made a choice, wouldn't you say?'

'Nonsense,' Jean says. 'It's not capable of choice. It was friendly enough with me. A new diversion, that's all. First the boat, then us, now him.'

All the same, she sounds resentful. Tony smiles.

'Come now,' he says. 'Jealous?'

'Of a dolphin? Don't be absurd.'

'Look at them now. Don't you think they make an attractive picture?'

Jean dries herself slowly and deliberately. She makes a point of not looking. But Tony cannot take his gaze away. He thinks, suddenly, his heart may be beating faster. The two in the water appear to be indulging in some curious skirmish. Then the boy half rises, a shiny brown, and with a startling smile. His face is altogether different. And Tony can see the boy is, after all, still a boy. He is almost out of the water entirely, supported by the dolphin, and Tony thinks he may be trying to get astride it. But he slips and falls, head first and legs wild. The dolphin appears to dive down and lightly bump him up to the surface again. The boy doesn't repeat the manoeuvre, to Tony's disappointment. He simply swims with it once more. And he is towed again.

Jean, dry, allows herself to look at last.

'He's not doing any more than I did,' she says. 'Less, if anything. Who is he, anyway?'

'A boy,' Tony replies, rather distracted.

'Clever. I'd never have guessed.'

'He lives here with his parents,' Tony continues unwillingly. 'Rather a solitary.'

'Dear God, not another problem child. He looked sulky enough.'

'His is rather special. His problem, I mean.'

'They always are, surely.'

'Distinctive, then. It seems he shot his sister last year.' Tony pauses. 'If he regrets anything, I'd say, it's probably that he didn't shoot himself too.'

Jean appears interested for the first time. At least her silence is impressive.

'You know him, then?' she asks finally.

'I've encountered him. This morning is really only the second time.' He sighs, realizing he will have to tell it all, almost. 'Funny thing is, I tried to interest him in the dolphin. But he wasn't having any. So it seems our friend the dolphin has just had a triumph of sorts. That's probably it, come to think. Probably why, if you want an answer. The boy is a challenge. We aren't. Or won't that do?'

Jean seems more mellow. 'They are,' she concedes, 'rather beautiful to watch.'

'True.'

'I was thinking of the dolphin as well as the boy.'

'So was I.'

'Tony . . .'

'Yes?'

'Sorry. That wasn't called for.'

'You're forgiven.'

'Why are you so terribly amiable?'

'Second nature. Or first line of defence.'

'You are, you know. You make me feel ashamed. Don't you dislike me on principle or something?'

'I have no principles,' he says. 'That's my trade secret. No unnecessary baggage.'

'How much do you dislike me personally, then?'

'I didn't say I did.'

'Then—'

'In point of fact, I don't.'

'What a morning,' she declares at length. 'My God.'

'Quite anomalous,' he agrees.

They look out upon the sea they have abandoned. It appears the boy and dolphin may never tire of each other. 'I was jealous,' she says. 'You were right.'

He finds her hand involved in his, quite tangibly, an unexpected offering. And somewhere to grip, after all; as solid as most things though possibly as evanescent.

'Of course,' he says. 'For all that it matters. I may have been too, and might be still.' Of whom, though, or what? He prefers, on the whole, not to decide.

'Tony, you're alone here. And I am. And we seem to get along. True?'

'True.'

'I've never been much good at offering anything except shelter.' She pauses. 'And company, for what that's worth.'

'Fair enough.' If he sounds vague, it is possibly because his gaze is still seaward. 'At our age, that's about it, surely.' As a general observation this, he thinks, is harmless and adequate enough, so far as he thinks about it at all. 'There can't be much more.'

'Tony, you don't understand.'

'No?' His tone is surprised. And her persistence is, in truth, astonishing enough. He cannot be irritated either, much as he might prefer to watch the figures in the sea without distraction.

'I want you to come back with me. To my place.'

It appears he must consider her hand after all. Possibly he is not superfluous, entirely. 'Now?'

'Now, Tony. Now. Please. Only now, if you like. But please, this once. Now.'

And he understands himself in some way committed at last, if not really when or how, even though he understands very little else of what has happened and what happens in the next few minutes. As they retreat from the shore he has the impression of people swarming untidily from everywhere, from behind trees and sandhills, out of suddenly open doors, down tracks, across the sand. Children, adults, the straggling old. The uproar grows behind, and then diminishes as they walk away from the beach. He wonders about the boy, and the dolphin. He doesn't doubt that the dolphin will clear off again. And the boy? But he doesn't have time to wonder for long. As soon as he is alone with Jean, her door not even shut, other things contend for attention. The demand in her thighs hardly surprises him, but his own response does. He is not in the slightest superfluous, and has never been less unreal. It is all so swift their striving toward release might appear some brutal game; moments later, though, they are like limp children after a race, quite wilted.

'Why did he shoot his sister?' Jean asks presently.

He doesn't understand for a moment. Then he does, entirely.

'I can't imagine,' he says.

That is the morning most people will remember, and speak about afterwards.

For example they may recall in detail the perfection of the morning itself. The sun flashing silver on the sea, glowing gold on the hills. The hugeness of the sky, the clarity of the air.

Just awoken, most people run clumsily, gropingly, into that spectacular morning, some in dressing-gowns, children in pyjamas and women with hair-curlers, men tucking in shirt-tails as they jog breathless to the beach. For the news has sped from house to house around the already alert bay. And when they arrive on the beach, that part of the beach where people are gathering from all over, they see more or less what they have been promised. The dolphin is gambolling near the shore with, of all people on the island, the Garland boy.

And when that morning is recalled, people will find it least easy to describe the indelibly luminous oddness of the scene, just how the dolphin looked with the boy. As large as life, many will say for want of more vivid phrase.

'He has made bloody thing a pet,' Frank Yakich says in wonder. 'Is now just a pet. Look.'

For now David Garland is slowly walking alongside the creature in shallow water, tickling, stroking, coaxing it forward.

'Stay back,' he calls. And most people do. It may be the memory of the disastrous rush the day before; it may also be because people are confused by the sudden morning and the marvel. Anyway they obey; they do stay back.

What happens then may be the thing most difficult to explain. For then, as they see, he wades to the beach and asks for children, any children. And the surprising thing is that children are surrendered to him, despite his being David Garland, and perhaps even because he is: people are still overcome by the strangeness; it is an odd morning and a year ago besides. The children themselves, of course, are willing enough to be carried out to the dolphin one by one. He holds each lightly upon its back while it cruises back and forward in shallow water. The dolphin does not appear to mind. Now and then there is a perhaps impatient flick of tail. Most children have a turn by the end. The remainder prefer, for the time being, to stay close to their mothers. The boy shoos away the few adults who approach too near. 'Another time,' he says firmly. His smile is seldom more than faint, and for the children. Another surprising thing, which may be more so in retrospect, is that no one disputes his standing with the dolphin.

When the last child has been borne ashore, squealing and chuckling, the boy swims out toward open sea with the dolphin. He is seen floating with it out in the bay for some time. There are some who will claim that he is talking to it out there. Finally they part. The dolphin speeds away and the boy swims in the direction of Hau headland.

The crowd takes an hour or more to disperse.

Zoe goes home with the Professor to prepare his breakfast. 'So we were wrong,' she says. For emphasis she bangs a pan upon the stove. 'Quite wrong.'

'In what way?' he asks.

'It was just looking for someone, all the time,' she explains vaguely. 'Like us. Just looking for someone. That's all. It's really no mystery, if you think about it.'

'No mystery, perhaps, if you're fanciful enough,' Professor Thomson observes. 'If you're fanciful enough there is never any mystery in anything.'

'But that's the point,' she says.

'The point?' he gropes.

'The point of being fanciful. What else?'

'You mean it helps?'

'And hurts. At times. It all depends.'

'Zoe,' he sighs, and shakes his head, 'here I was starting to think you might be good for me.'

'You could try.'

'Try what?'

'Being fanciful again. Not just for a change. For good; for real.'

'It's rather late in the day.'

'Does anything else help, then?' she asks.

'A certain amount of faith in things as they are,' he says after a time. 'Otherwise . . .'

'Yes?' she persists. 'Otherwise?'

'Otherwise,' he concedes, 'there is nothing.'

'And what have you got, after all this time?'

'Nothing,' he says. 'Or next to nothing. You know that. Or ought to, by now.'

'Then you can try. What have you got to lose? Nothing. Really nothing.' She starts cracking one egg after another into the pan. 'There,' she says, 'I think a dozen should be enough. For an omelette for two. My cooking's not the best, so I may as well be on the safe side. Quantity if not quality.'

She looks at him quickly. He still sits quiet, as if he hasn't heard. She gives attention to the pan again. It is some time before he speaks.

'The odd thing is,' he remarks, 'I thought you came to me for help.'

'I did,' she agrees. 'But it isn't as easy as I thought.'

'No?'

'No. Because you need help to help. Even if it's only me cooking breakfast.'

'I see.'

'Or a bit more. I don't know yet how much more.'

'And then I'll be able to help you?'

'More or less. Yes.'

He shakes his head again, but more decisively. 'Then it is too late in the day. Far too late.'

'Too late?' she cries mockingly. 'It's hardly even morning.'

'Why do you misunderstand me?'

'Because I have to.'

After a while she starts to serve up the blackened wreckage of the omelette.

'So I can understand,' she adds quietly.

THIRTEEN

It is certainly a morning Ben Blackwood will remember.

In the afternoon of the day before, after seeing the dolphin for the first time, he walked to Te Hianinu's vineyard where he spent much time sampling and buying wine. In the evening, upon his overloaded return home, he drank himself to sleep. He doesn't wake until sometime after three in the morning. He can't tell the time: his watch has stopped at three. But it is still dark. The acid wine has left his mouth foul and his head throbs. He carries his self-inflicted wounds into the warm night, which is lightening faintly in the east, and relieves himself in long grass. Then he returns inside the cottage to make himself black coffee and toast. He is surprised by his hunger, even more surprised by the clarity of his thoughts as he sits alone in the night.

For everything is so obvious, so simple. He has followed a trail which, if spurious, has at times been quite splendid in its lunacy. And reversing every signpost on his way, for symmetry's sake, he has arrived at the only end possible, a dead end. The wonder is that it has taken him so long to see.

Imaginatively at least, he can follow the trail back. Well, as far back as that Easter in London—what year? Somewhere in mid-century, when his world still had coherence. Seven years ago, or eight, perhaps nearly nine. Long enough. The Aldermaston march. The last day, Easter Monday. The marchers coming in from all over London, cascading colourfully across the grass of Turnham Green. The ranks forming for the last nine-mile plod to Trafalgar Square.

He was surprised to find himself there, and wouldn't have been but for Sheila. She went alone to join the marchers on Good Friday, the first day, when they set out for London from the gates of nuclear war. Easter Saturday and Sunday were taken up with a long-promised trip into the country, and it was on her insistence that he went to join the marchers on the last day. He wasn't cynical about it all, despite what Sheila said: he just needed, for good personal reasons, to keep his distance. And that was difficult enough, with Sheila. She was from South Africa, a political expatriate. They met and mated in London, but never quite married, when Ben was still reasonably left-wing. There were no complications then. Sheila was a large healthy girl, long-haired and long-limbed, as vigorous in speech as in body; she had a statuesque quality which turned even the most casual domestic stance into something dramatic. He thought himself, on the whole, equal to her discontent. True, he couldn't always share it imaginatively—after all, he'd never seen Africa and knew its sorrows only second-hand, and felt at home in London as she never did. He couldn't always share her friends either, though he tried: other exiled liberals and leftists from South Africa. Organizational squabbles and rather petty conspiracy appeared to obsess them. And there was something depressingly guilt-ridden even about the best of them. Ben understood why, or thought he did, but that didn't mean he found them any more appealing as people.

Still, he rubbed along. He never objected to Sheila filling their flat with her friends. She had her own life, at least her own past. He had his own, if it came to that, but it counted less as years in London passed. Ben styled himself an outsider only when it was convenient. Most of the time he might have been a Londoner born. Most of the time he never thought of himself as anything else. It was only in midnight depressions, or when things were going badly, either with Sheila or his work, that he remembered his birth in the South Pacific, and the fragment of childhood spent there; at these times he would polish the fragment until it glowed, outshining the present, his surroundings and his disappointments. Only in adversity was it ever important, and then more as lucky charm, like his mother's pendant, an ancestral Maori image carved in greenstone, which he was given after her death. He could remember being happy in another place: that was the simple magic of the thing. And it wasn't something to share with Sheila. She had enough nostalgia for both of them. He made something of the fact that he was really an outsider in London when he first met Sheila. But never since then. Anyway he hadn't much to share. There was actually little to remember.

His father, an engineer, went out to New Zealand after some unhappy love affair between the wars to work on a large civil construction project. In a remote country district where he worked, he met the attractive girl who was to become Ben's mother. She was part-Maori, lively and loving, and possibly too vital for Ben's father. But he married her, presumably because Ben was already on his way into the world. The marriage evidently tied his father to the distant country; perhaps he didn't like the idea of taking his wife back to face England. He took one job after another, most of them unworthy of his skills, in different parts of New Zealand; when the depression struck he took what he could get anywhere.

Ben's recall of these years was faint and confused, if happy. He was far closer to his mother than to his father, who often lived and worked far from home. When he tried to recall particulars, Ben seldom could. And then, later, something would dislodge and fall into his consciousness at a moment of crisis; but stray pebbles rather than an avalanche. He could remember hills, a river, his mother's lightly steering hand on his shoulder, strange trees he had never seen since and could still not name; and then, for example, a seascape, tawny limbs of land, shiny rocks and high-flying gulls, a sunlit sea and a sandy shore, and he dawdled wondering at his own footprints, hand in hand with his mother, always warm and soft beside him. It was more this he remembered, pressed images, rather than anything important. His father's homesickness, for example; he recalled nothing of that. The only obstacle to his father's return was removed when Ben's mother died in a sanatorium. Ben was just seven when taken off to England by his father. Mr Blackwood's colonial adventure was over, but he had Ben as awkward souvenir.

It wasn't a question of colour: Ben's fraction of Maori blood, something less than half and something more than a quarter, was never especially prominent. He could easily be mistaken for half-Arab, part-Jew, Eurasian, or just dark Welsh. Ben could just as easily have forgotten it entirely, though his sometimes wistful father reminded him of it with frequency in later life. He sent Ben off to one school after another. And Ben, always a misfit with an odd accent, detested all of them. His father married again, and in time Ben learned to manage the idea of a stepmother. His mother had become just a memory of warmth, though even this could still help his way through bleak corridors and classrooms, help him survive those almost friendless schools. His rebellions grew quieter, shrewder. He graduated from the Communist Party while still at Oxford, but when he began work as a journalist he remained coolly committed to the far left. That was how things were when he met Sheila. She said it was a wonder to her that someone so vastly and engagingly clumsy could talk and write with such precision. This was not strictly true, at least about his precision, but there was no real need to argue so fine a point, not with a girl like Sheila.

People rather than events changed him. It became clear that politics were too serious to be taken seriously. He borrowed his ironic perspective from friends in Eastern Europe when he began travelling there on assignments. To take politics too seriously was to risk insanity, and he saw enough insanity to clinch the argument, so far as he was concerned. Where once his world view had been of clash of ideologies, now he saw the struggle as the human race versus all ideology. On the one side was prospect of survival, on the other there was none. He was, however, quite prepared to concede that this view might be necessary for his personal survival. Or his personal sanity, something to which he barely clung after his experience in Hungary. Yet it seemed to him possible that the human race might still muddle through. Even ideologists were human, unlikely though it appeared at times, and that was a foothold in the enemy camp.

All this led, of course, to conflict with Sheila. On a high-minded plane, naturally; as if to prove Ben's argument their relationship, in bed and at table, survived on a purely human level. For Sheila's friends it was simple. 'Ben's sold out,' they told her. 'You've got to face it.'

Useless for Ben to observe that they, if they hadn't forgotten it, had been battling an ideology, white supremacy, in the name of simple humanity. Useless for him to point out that the struggle was more or less the same everywhere. It seemed they had to have one ideology in exchange for another, or nothing. In the end they might have nothing, with a vengeance. It all depressed him. Even Sheila, to his dismay, would never hear him out.

'You're trying to make a virtue out of it, a religion out of complete passivity,' she declared. 'That's what it amounts to.' Clearly passivity would never suit Sheila in any sense. 'Sometimes I wonder if they're right, if it isn't true that you've sold out. Either that or you're a holy fool, Ben. I prefer to believe the latter, for the time being.'

'The time being?'

'Take it any way you like,' she sniffed.

'If only you'd stop to listen,' he pleaded.

'And hear what?'

'Anything. Just listening would be a start. I don't mean just to me; to anything.'

'I've heard all I want to hear about your purity.'

'It's not a question of purity. It's a question of staying alive.'

Yet he had Sheila still, though this was no longer anything in which he could take much pride. Soon doors were shut on much of Sheila's life. Ben wished for a child. It wasn't because a child would bring the dusty, long irrelevant question of marriage down from the shelf. A child might offer a better chance to meet. Bed itself was hardly adequate. Often, when Ben had been working hard, and Sheila involved mysteriously, that was literally the only place where they did meet. And even that could be grim enough, with Sheila bitter and ashamed of her own weakness; he could take no pleasure himself in seeing her helpless before the need of flesh. She wanted cruelty, it seemed, and not just conquest. He could not offer even a half-hearted facsimile of cruelty, though perhaps even that might have been insufficient for her discontents.

Out of it, anyway, Ben spun first one tale, then another. He took as motto something he found in Isak Dinesen: 'All sorrows can be borne if you put them into a story or tell a story about them.' People, however, seemed not to find the sorrows at all. 'A brisk, gusty comedy of life among London's expatriates,' said a Sunday reviewer of his first novel. 'Quite as comic as his first,' said the same reviewer of his second. 'Mr Blackwood just can't put a foot wrong. The measured solemnity of his prose throws into sharp relief the abrasive absurdity of his situations.'

So much for his precision. And Isak Dinesen was wrong. Sheila was still there, no less easily borne. More distant than ever, since the books. 'It's typical of you,' was almost all she said by way of criticism, 'to stand off and laugh.'

'Laugh?' he said in dismay. Yet in the end it seemed laughter might be the only thing left.

Anyway he was committed to his perverse kind of success now. He had a reputation for it. A tightwire walker, he could see no end to the wire in gloom and shadow, and he dared not look down, where the lights flared.

Then Easter Monday, and the ranks forming on Turnham Green, under the anti-bomb banners.

Until that point exactly, he had coasted; it was up to Sheila to choose, if she liked. Since she didn't, he coasted.

'Let's find the international contingents,' she said, pushing among the thousands. Her eyes shone.

They passed the Americans, Canadians, Germans, Australians and West Indians; and came, of course, to the South Africans. There was hardly a face unfamiliar. 'I think I'll have a look around,' said Ben quickly.

'A what?'

'A look around. It'll be another half-hour before this lot moves. Or more.'

'You'll be back?' she said.

'I expect I will be.'

He looked back as he walked away. Sheila had fallen into the ranks between two bearded compatriots. Both were talking to her earnestly, and others were gathering. Sheila gestured with vigour as she spoke. A queen bee among her swarm.

Ben actually didn't get far; no further than a small blonde girl struggling to unfurl a banner. 'Can I help?' he asked. 'Who are you?'

'At the moment,' she said, 'I'm the New Zealand contingent. And, yes, you can help. Thanks. Just pull it that way, gently. That's it. And could you hold on to it, for a bit? So people can see. There's bound to be a New Zealander along in a minute to take your place.'

'Well, actually,' Ben said, 'it just so happens—'

He found himself banner-bound without even thinking about it. He supposed Sheila wouldn't miss him, particularly; she had more than enough company. And he thought no more about it. Yet if ever there was a decision, or choice made, that was probably it.

'And you've never been back?' the girl said chattily.

'Never,' Ben said. 'And it doesn't seem likely.'

By that time a couple of dozen New Zealanders had been drawn by the banner. The forward columns were beginning to move.

'You're going to stay with us, then?' the girl said.

'I'll keep up the number.'

'There'll be more as we go along. I've some art student friends joining at Hammersmith.'

'An art student yourself?'

'Drama.'

As the international column started to move, to the sound of the West Indian steel band, there was a bonus of another dozen New Zealanders. Ben no longer really had excuse for staying. There were more than enough willing hands for the banner he clutched; and the number of marchers was no longer entirely discreditable to a country he found it hard to imagine. The lively little blonde girl, though, was real enough.

'It hasn't been bad,' she was saying. 'This is my second year. I don't know what I'm going to do yet. And what do you do, by the way?'

He almost repeated, bitterly, the first words to mind: Stand off and laugh, so I hear. Instead he mumbled something noncommital.

'Oh,' the girl laughed. 'I might have guessed. People like you seem two a penny in London.'

'One a penny,' he said. 'Inflation.'

'And what do you write about?'

'One a penny people.'

'I might have guessed that too. It's really as much a fishbowl as anywhere else, London, isn't it? Just more crowded with fish of the same colour. I don't think I'm going to stay.'

'Why not?'

'Too cosy. Too many people like myself. Not enough real people. I mean, I can understand most people like me enjoying that. It's just I don't, much.'

'But what about your career?'

'I don't think I've much of a career anyway. Not here, or back there. But I enjoy myself, regardless.'

'I'm sure you do.'

It wasn't difficult for Ben to enjoy himself either, that day. The atmosphere was festive, the music gay. The marchers were colourful, and the roads sunlit. A pleasant enough way of protesting the death of the world. Above all, conversation with the girl was less effort than any he had known for a long time.

He had come, more or less, as penance. So his amiable mood surprised him. Hammersmith, Earls Court, Kensington High, Hyde Park; and then, after five hours, the long silent tramp up Whitehall to the square. It wasn't until he saw the thousands filling the square, the columns dissolving, that he thought about finding Sheila again.

Of course he failed to find her, though he searched for an hour, around the crowd and through its centre, under the booming speeches and scattering pigeons and warm blue sky out of which nuclear fire might rage. One person among fifty thousand; it was hopeless.

But he did find the New Zealand banner again, and the little blonde actress furling it as the square began to empty. 'You look lost,' she observed.

He didn't arrive home until after eleven that night.

'I don't believe you marched at all,' Sheila said. He had found her sitting alone in the flat. Unwashed glasses in the kitchen indicated she had done some entertaining after the march too.

'Of course I did,' he said, pouring himself coffee. 'With a different group, that's all. With the New Zealanders, as a matter of fact.'

'What new affectation is this, Ben?'

'No affectation. I was born there, if you remember.'

'Ben, you're no more a New Zealander than I'm an Eskimo. And don't tell me they've been marching till this hour. They ought to be half way to Paris by now.'

'Please yourself,' Ben said. 'I couldn't find you, so I went off to a pub.'

The lie was the first of importance he had ever told Sheila.

'You must have known I'd be having friends around afterwards.'

'I suppose that should have crossed my mind.' Quite inadequate, of course; he had never been able to lie with much verve anyway. 'It's just that I was caught up with these people.'

'What people?'

'These people I marched with.'

'With whom you have so much in common, I suppose?'

'They're people.'

'They must have been very honoured. Ben Blackwood, the author, keeping them company. Was that it, Ben? Big frog in a small puddle? That it?'

'Look. Sheila, let's call it quits. All right?'

He supposed he gave Sheila her chance then. Her last chance, though that was not in his mind; but she wanted to keep the boulder rolling. It was not difficult. It was just that she had no idea of what else she was about to dislodge. No more than he, if it came to that.

'And you bought them all drinks,' she said, 'and you struck the pose of the successful colonial who's made it with the Sunday papers? That right? New Zealand, Ben? I doubt if you could even name the capital city.'

'Auckland,' he said, 'or perhaps Wellington. One or the other. One's the biggest, the other's the capital. One or the other anyway. Not that it matters.'

Sheila laughed. 'You really are incredible. Even I know better.'

'Well, actually,' he began defensively, and then heard himself say, 'I've been thinking of going out there.'

'You've what?' He seemed to have got past Sheila's guard at last; he could hardly leave off now.

'Been thinking of going out there. For a trip.'

'Since when?'

'On and off, for some time now.' In fact, for all of ten seconds.

'You're not serious.'

'Why not?' He took a deep breath and launched himself upon the new lie. 'Journalistically, I've gone stale on Eastern Europe. Each trip the same old routine, the same run-around, the same questions.'

'And what's New Zealand going to do for you?'

'It depends.'

'Nothing happens there.'

'That might be the point.'

'My God,' she said, 'you're going quite beyond reason.'

'There might be some articles in it. Some of the other Pacific islands too. Fiji, for example. What do you know about Fiji? How do you know nothing happens there? Or Samoa?'

'You'll be telling me Tahiti next.'

'Well, why not? I seem to recall riots there recently. That might interest even you.' He seemed perilously near some point of commitment. The thin, rather drab little fiction began to take on colour and some substance. 'The world doesn't turn around Africa, you know. Or London, come to that.'

'Our man Robert Louis Blackwood reporting from the beaches of the South Pacific. Ben, it's really too much. Which ear will you wear your flower behind, Ben? I rather think the right would suit.'

'You seem,' he said sombrely, 'to forget my Polynesian blood.'

'All two pints of it, Ben?'

'All three pints of it. I had the idea that might have excited you once—the blood, and my colour.'

It had just slipped out with no thought of consequence: half a joke, no more. And half an amiably tired defence. But Sheila was on her feet.

'You bastard,' she said. 'You filthy, filthy bastard.'

'But—'

'You have gone rotten, Ben. Rotten right through.'

'I just—'

'To come out with something like that. A squalid bit of—racist filth. To call it by its mildest name.'

'Racist?' he said. 'But it's me who—' He sat paralysed, helpless with the knowledge not only that he had gone too far but that he had also, unexpectedly, found himself in an area of truth. 'Never mind. I'm sorry. I didn't mean—'

'You never mean anything, Ben. Anything. But it adds up, all the same.'

'Sheila, we're both tired. Let's forget it.'

But the forgetting was past, that was clear. The forgetting, and much else perhaps. They still, stabbing back and forward, had to find out how much else.

'You arrive home dishevelled at damn near midnight and ramble on about going to the South Pacific. Then you say forget it.'

'London's got me down. Perhaps that's it. I'm thinking about a book too.' His reviving invention surprised and dismayed him. 'I've about played out the London scene. Fictionally, I mean. A trip away, a new perspective, might do me good.'

'You're played out,' she said. 'Not London. You know you haven't written a word of that new book in months. And you've never been very serious about it all anyway. It's all been a game to you, a cheap little game, and you've never pretended otherwise. You drew a lucky ticket in the publishing lottery—and had one or two good connections on the literary pages. So you're not going to sit there and tell me you're going all that way to boost your literary reputation, whatever that happens to be at the moment. Nil, I imagine. You were last year's novelty.'

Since they'd started the truth game, they might as well play it out. Or she could play it out: he was too tired, too depressed; too hopeless. He had overdrawn on his reserves, somewhere along the way, and his account was empty of irony now; he had lost all distance from himself. It was even conceivable that Sheila might be able to hurt him. And that hadn't happened in a long time.

'Look,' he said. 'Why pretend? We've had two lives, two separate lives, for a long time now. And whether I go or stay shouldn't mean a great deal to you any more. If it does, say so now.'

For the first time that evening, she had nothing to say.

'So that's it,' he said, getting to his feet. It would have been different, he thought, if he had posed the challenge in bed. But that would have been unfair, and would he have got truth anyway? 'I don't even really need to think it over much. I'll go.'

He had, it appeared, found his solution. All this from a flighty blonde actress with a banner, and two or three not very satisfactory hours in her arms. Likely he would never see the girl again. Idiotic, if he stopped to think; and comic. And too sad for tears. He seemed never to make a real decision in his life; he just blundered upon them among the debris of doubt. The South Pacific, New Zealand? The idea terrified him even as he rushed to embrace it.

Perhaps morning would make it seem quaint and entirely absurd. On the other hand, this evening he wasn't drunk for once. And he could almost believe now that the idea had been astir for a long time, it seemed so logical. So ideal a solution. He brushed past Sheila on his way to the kitchen and another cup of coffee. Better coffee than making a virtually confessional grab for the whisky.

'Ben—'

Did she have, after all, something to say? He turned at the kitchen door. A certain shading of her voice could still, not surprisingly, disclose an excessive weakness in his body. And there was some tension in her stance too, as her hands gripped the back of a chair, her body arched.

'You're not serious,' she stated.

'Suppose I am? Look, it's not impossible for me to get back, you know. It's not the far side of the moon.'

'It's far enough. But you're not serious; I can tell.'

So he found himself, far sooner than he would have liked, past the point of commitment. If Sheila were ever to take him seriously, he would have to go. If ever he were to possess a certain minimum of self-respect. The last two reasons he would have cared to claim. He would far sooner have offered himself something sentimentally simple, such as: There's a beach where I walked once, with my mother. I'd like to walk it again, if I can find it. To see if it's as perfect as I remember; and the sky as bright.

And that proposition, he discovered with a twinge, was real enough too. Too real. Another weakness, least expected.

'I'm serious, all right,' he said quietly. 'So were you going to say something?'

'Nothing. Never mind.'

And if she had something to say, it was left unsaid. For the notion did not seem quaint the next morning, or the morning after, for that matter, when he booked his passage. And when it came to packing, and goodbye, it might have been another trip into Europe; it was just that his bags were fatter than usual, and there were more of them.

'How long, Ben?' she finally asked.

'It could be a year,' he said. 'But there's no point in making promises. Unless you want me to make them.'

She was tight-lipped. He could hear the faint, endless sound of London's traffic.

'All right,' he said. 'So that's it. Look after yourself.'

'I'll have to,' she said, 'won't I?'

It seemed later that he probably misunderstood that too; like so much else. For it sounded more a threat than a cry for help. But what if he had understood? Would it have been any different? Perhaps, by that stage, he hadn't wanted to understand; he might have wanted a threat, a sexual taunt, rather than an appeal. For his out; for his peace of mind.

'Anyway,' she added, 'you're the one who most needs to look after yourself. Wait and see. Things are sometimes real, Ben—really real, horribly real, beyond a joke.'

He wasn't, as it turned out, to have his peace of mind long anyway.

He had been gone less than six months, still directionless after the shock of farewelling his seven years with Sheila, when he read of a place in South Africa called Sharpeville. Bodies split by bullets lay awry under the African sun; the blurred cable pictures seemed only to add to the horror of the massacre. Those dark heaps of torn flesh in the dust; the dapper police with automatic weapons. He could imagine how Sheila felt, or thought he could. It was all real; how could he ever have been fool enough to doubt it? That pettiness toward Sheila and her friends at last seemed unforgivable. For in some of the cable pictures were other people—not the dead and dying in the dust, not the police with efficient faces; but the grey ones, the indifferent ones, the spectators. He could, if he tried, recognize himself among them. Contrite, he began searching for words to put in a letter to Sheila, but was too slow finding them.

Her letter arrived before his was mailed; and his, in the end, was never mailed. She didn't mention Sharpeville, or anything else much outside their domestic world, though the rest of the world was there, a steady drumming, behind her words. It was no use, she said, the way things were. If they were going to break, they should break cleanly. Not leave room for anything like hope to linger. The fact was, she didn't want Ben back. And she was, besides, going home to South Africa. Obviously, she added, it would be inadvisable, not to say uncomfortable, for him to follow.

That last, he thought, was rather unnecessary. But he was not entirely sure he saw the rest of her meaning. He saw, if he saw anything, a flash of bullets, blood, dust, sunlight. Would she have gone home if he hadn't left her? That was something he might live with for ever, if he weren't careful, and he knew no way to be careful. But he could see that they had, after all, been nesting in no-man's land.

He envisaged her stepping off her boat, under the African sun. Until that point imagination was under no strain.

Thereafter, in imagination, he had to live with a different Sheila. He never received another letter from her. But it wasn't to be too long before he heard a great deal about her, in a public way. A lunatic bomb exploded, prematurely, in some part of Johannesburg; and arrests were made. The first news reports were vague about the people involved. A police statement alleged the conspirators belonged to a London-based terrorist group. Ben felt helpless tension for days, then weeks. He had no way of confirming anything. He had no address for Sheila.

When the trial began, she appeared as witness for the state.

Her evidence convicted three young men. One of them Ben remembered clearly as visitor to the London flat. He always appeared such a nervous, nondescript individual; one of Sheila's hangers-on. Had Sheila ever slept with him? For he seemed one of the most likely contenders for Ben's place in her bed, when Ben left. Never really a contender for the gallows. Defence counsel tried to discredit Sheila's tangled testimony; it was pointed out that Sheila had for some time been under considerable police pressure to turn state's witness against her friends. London newspapers stressed her evident demoralization in the witness box, and editorially discussed allegations of torture.

Sheila, in return for services to the state, received only a nominal prison sentence. Her three friends were considered fortunate to escape with life sentences.

Then silence. A silence more profound when all the letters Ben wrote, care of every likely address, were returned one by one. Finally her courtroom lawyer wrote to say his client wished no communication. And there was never anything else to learn, apart from a single-column story, little more than a belated footnote to a now half-forgotten trial, in a London Sunday paper. Headed *Tragedy of a Witness,* it told among other things how Sheila had made two known suicide attempts after her release from prison, and had finally been admitted to mental hospital for treatment as a drug addict.

And Ben? Ben was left with what he had begun. Years later, too many years later, he is still left with it. His lucky charm, the country of his half-remembered childhood, is after all his life. He has rubbed it, polished it, a hundred times in a hundred stories. He still supposes, from time to time, that he is going back to London, though it becomes more difficult to convince himself. For no one writes, any more, to ask is he coming back; there is no one to argue with, now, but himself He has written almost all he is ever likely to write about Fiji and Samoa; even Tahiti. And New Zealand too, for that matter, though he has gone from one beach to another, and never yet found the place where he innocently wondered at his own first footprints.

Yet it is either that or walk the streets he once walked with Sheila. His escape, though not intended, has seemed entire. Perhaps he hasn't found the place he walked with his mother because he has looked in vain for the wild, strange and lonely; that beach is possibly smothered by split-level ranch-style homes, with prickly plants thick in their gardens, and crazy-paved pathways. Anyway he has all but abandoned the mystery. He continues to confect books for his publishers. He has found it fairly simple to parody his own early style; to repeat the tricks, go through the hoops. He can, using that style as net, deliver up tourists in Tahiti, colonials in Fiji, beachcombers on Rarotonga, bushmen in New Zealand. His reputation may be small, since he lost his London literary connections, but it isn't unprofitable. For a long time he has been able to continue in paralysed parody as if nothing had ever happened. And even able to wonder, without dent or crack in his reality, if Sheila is still really alive. Or whether she ever was; or himself.

He has tried cities, at times, for company or something like it, and now and then, in some bed or other, has found a passable facsimile. There is just sufficient of an underground society for comfort; hardly anyone in this country knows him as anything but an English drifter. Anonymity, in fact, has always been the least of his problems; it was once his advantage over other journalists in Eastern Europe, in days remote. He fades quick into crowds.

The last time in the city, though, he was earnestly pestered by a regular and otherwise unsurprising friend of the night who wished to know how he felt about, of all places, Vietnam. She even, incredibly, imagined he might walk beside her in some demonstration. In panic, finding himself unable to settle to a fresh book, he fled to a new half-way house on Motutangi. For a time he has known a certain comfort. A trip to the city presents no demand; and he can, if something is worth prolonging, bring a companion back to the island. This isn't often, as it happens; but then his trips to the city are of decreasing frequency anyway. He has finished one book, shakily, and begun another for lack of any better idea. The thought of new travel, or any shift at all, leaves him with nausea. But now the problem of avoiding the world has become as great an obsession as the world itself: now and then he is still able to see lucidly, and reassuringly, that Vietnam is after all just a synonym, and symptom. Yet because of his isolation, as if from infection, the fever has finally found him in most virulent form; he has no resistance at all. His typewriter has begun to lose its regular tick in the mornings. Now it is seldom heard at any time, though he attacks it often enough.

He can cash cheques on his London bank and see himself as twentieth-century remittance-man, the last of the breed, while his money lasts.

He can catch fish and grow vegetables.

He can look at the sea.

And he can continue to observe his quaint private rituals—burning cigarettes before a typewriter, buying no newspapers.

The next best thing might be to purchase his passage back to Europe, if he can find the money, and see what happens. This proposition he still entertains, however little he finds it entertaining, when he has the mental energy. For when he makes an effort he sees himself fitfully at one with this vague society in the south, flung off from Europe, a pale particle of energy, burning out. To become an irrelevant outpost, a stranded people. At times he can imagine the country being given back without grief to Polynesia again, the ruins of its forsaken cities testimony to the advance and retreat of Western man.

Such self-dramatization can help only so far; certainly not as far as the office of a travel agent. It is almost as if he has to see what happens, or won't happen, to convince himself; but summer ignites no decision.

What does happen finally, improbably, is noise drifting up from the beach, up the hill to his cottage, and into his hungover morning. This time he is not too late.

Two hours after the dolphin has gone back to sea he is still walking up and down the beach. It seems he is talking to people.

FOURTEEN

The dolphin reappears in the afternoon. It cruises the length of the bay, fifty to a hundred yards out from shore. There are still people on the beach from morning. Many of them rush clothed into the water, calling out—though whether to their fellows or to the dolphin is not clear. Drinkers from the pub follow, some still with glasses in their hands, since the pub has an alert look-out now. The school empties fifteen minutes before the final bell, teachers following the children. Shops slam shut. Even Miss Murch, the lanky postmistress, is seen gambolling to a vantage point. Before long, one way and another, most people in the bay are either on the run or in the water.

Zoe reaches the water's edge ahead of most, with Professor Thomson still some way behind. Around her the crowd billows.

A red-nosed old man she has not seen before grips her shoulder as he wobbles. 'Get it,' he wheezes, with a boozy smell. 'Somebody get it. Bring it back again. I never seen it this morning.'

'It is not within my powers,' Zoe answers politely. 'Though I should like very much to help, of course.'

The creature, meantime, remains aloof from shore.

The Professor at last stands beside her. He pants slightly. 'I am afraid it will not come,' she tells him. 'And people will be disappointed again.'

The red-nosed man is up to the knees of his trousers in the water, his face miserable.

But the photographer from the newspaper, who has just flown in, is going mad with a telescopic lens. He has spare film between his teeth as he wades.

Maurice Shadbolt

There are people trying to swim out toward the dolphin, but the distance is too great for most. And the creature shifts so fast besides.

'We need that boy again,' Zoe observes. 'Or the dolphin does.'

Someone is in distress, spluttering and sinking. Better swimmers have to make a rescue, forgetting the dolphin.

'Fantastic,' the Professor murmurs. 'I think they are all touched by sun. Or worse.'

'I would find the boy if I could,' Zoe continues.

'Lord knows what they think they're after,' he says.

'If I only knew where to begin finding him,' Zoe finishes. 'Otherwise people may drown.'

'Where are you going?' he asks quickly.

But Zoe has gone without another word. She walks along the shore, peering into faces. She is never noticed; eyes are distant. After a time she comes to a man and woman she recognizes. They have only just arrived on the beach, and are shedding towels and sandals.

'I'm sure you know the boy,' she announces without preliminary. 'If you are his friends, you must get him.'

'Good God,' Jean says, 'what's the matter now?' The odd girl rather alarms and confuses her, speaking with such vehemence.

'You must,' says Zoe, 'tell him the dolphin's waiting there.'

The man, however, appears to understand. 'I know who you mean,' he says gently. 'But we don't really know him at all.'

'Then who does?'

'That,' says the man, 'is an interesting question. But I can't help. Sorry. We're just going to swim out to it ourselves, if we can.'

They run into the water together. Dismayed, Zoe walks back, through the crowd, to the Professor. 'It's no good,' she says. 'I can't find him.'

'Who?' he asks vaguely.

'The boy, of course.'

'Boy?'

'The boy this morning.'

'Of course. Yes.'

'I don't think anyone else really saw him,' she says. 'Or cares. At least I'm starting to wonder.'

Now Frank Yakich is chugging in his launch to the dolphin. And from other directions the two swimmers, the man and woman, are

136

converging. The dolphin is the best part of two hundred yards out now and difficult to see, except when it frolics.

Excitement remains loud, nevertheless. There are cars arriving from more distant parts of the island, and doors crashing.

Elsewhere on the beach Ben Blackwood holds his breath. For it can't possibly happen again, though he hopes.

Harry Green watches through binoculars from his front veranda. 'There's not a house in the bay that wouldn't be easy to rob right now,' he tells his wife. He can see the woman racing to the shore, in a minute, if she doesn't control herself. 'Except ours,' he adds.

The swimmers and Frank Yakich, between them, appear to make little impression on the dolphin. It seems prepared to play, but not to shift nearer land. The cries from shore become shriller. For the afternoon is starting to escape.

Then there is a single swimmer, from somewhere in the direction of Hau headland, closing with the dolphin. For a time, perhaps, this figure is only visible to Zoe, who finally tugs Professor Thomson's arm. 'See?' she says in the noise. The first change most people see is in the dolphin itself, leaping high and streaking. After a time it is circling, closer and closer to shore, with the boy. The two adults and Frank Yakich trail behind in convoy.

Then the morning begins again.

There is one difference, though. The difference is in the strange girl no one really knows, who walks, wades, and finally swims, rather poorly, through the crowd to greet the boy. And then, while saying quiet things to the boy, also makes way for him—and the dolphin—by telling people to be careful and to move back. Since the girl appears to know what she is doing, people do move back; there is no one to suggest otherwise.

The newspaper photographer seems quite off his head now. For children are astride the dolphin again, and he is out of film.

The man and woman help the girl control the crowd, since someone has to, and lead children to the dolphin. The din is immense, but the creature remains calm, so long as the boy's arm rests about its head.

Some children laugh. Some weep. Some sit petrified and entirely expressionless upon the dolphin's back.

When the children are finished, it is the turn of the old. Who come close to see, but then have to touch, perhaps to lend their sometimes capricious sight conviction. The crippled are helped through the water; the blind are led; and the half-dead and dying are carried.

All have to touch. That is when the touching really begins.

An old lady with skinny legs, arthritic hands and silvercapped walking-stick is the first to cry out. 'It is electric,' she calls, to those who will hear. 'I could feel it all the way through my body, deep down.'

Someone recalls that her husband has been dead ten years.

But when she regains the sand, in her sopping costume, her eyes wide and wild, she throws down her walking-stick, totters free of helping hands, wanders shakily a few yards, and then falls to her knees in evident prayer.

It may be a miracle, if more is needed. The noise of the crowd has been slowly ebbing anyway. And now the sobs of the woman are for all to hear, as she prays.

'Jesus Christ,' says the fat honeymooner. 'I feel queer all through myself, just seeing.'

'Queer?' his wife giggles. 'You?'

Her giggling stops, though, when she sees his face. 'I'm gunna touch the bloody thing myself,' he announces, and lurches away.

'Bill,' she cries. 'Wait.'

But Bill is not much good at waiting. Nor, now, are most of those who have not touched. The crowd starting to thresh through the sea with new energy is no longer one of faces; it is arms, hands, fingers.

And it appears a frightening, tentacled thing from where Zoe stands, with the boy and the dolphin. Their two friends, the man and the woman, burst apart under the pressure, and are no longer a protection. In fact they are all but underfoot in moments.

The hands are everywhere.

'I think it is dangerous now,' she says urgently to the boy. 'I think you must go, take it away. I think—'

Before Zoe, still much given to thinking, has time to say more, the boy has launched himself away from the crowd, and the dolphin, perhaps with relief, is leaping after.

She swims a little way after them, before she is tired, with her clothing pulling her under. So she turns back to face the cheated people.

They are, after all, surprisingly mild and give her no attention at all.

For they are watching the boy, out in the bay, with the dolphin. The pair are up to their morning tricks, and more. The creature shoots clean from the water, several times, about the boy, in flashing streamers of spray.

The man takes Zoe's arm to help her from the sea. 'My name's Tony,' he says. 'You're a brave kid. It must have been like facing a rugby charge, all alone.'

He is a most gentle man, and his fingers encourage.

'I was afraid for the boy,' she states, since it perhaps has to be said. 'Everything could have been spoiled.'

'Of course,' he says, 'and it almost was. But I think the boy may be tough enough. Can I help you find your friend?'

'My friend?'

'The old fellow.'

'Yes,' she agrees, 'I expect he is my friend. It is just difficult for me to think, at the moment.'

Her head is tired, and her body still reeling. She rests comfortably against the man, who does not mind.

'I thought he might be your father,' the man remarks. 'I wondered.'

'Professor Thomson?'

'He looks old enough. Or your grandfather.'

'I wish . . .' she begins, and then finishes, 'It is a shame, in a way, he is not. Like, I mean, or more like.'

'Oh?'

'Anyway,' she says, 'he is definitely not my father. If that is all you wish to know.'

Out in the bay the boy and the dolphin continue to perform. So involved with each other it is almost indecent to watch.

'I'll go looking for him myself,' she adds, 'in a minute.' For she is grateful just to be held, for a bit.

The crowd is static and fairly quiet, but for a few cries from children and the sobs of the old woman, no longer praying, and now being comforted by friends. They are insisting, it appears, on the return of her walking-stick, which she will not have.

'All the same,' Zoe says, 'we should look after them, the way we did. Otherwise . . .'

'Yes?'

But Zoe finds it difficult to think past the word 'otherwise'. It seems there is nothing past it. 'I suppose I mean,' she continues, 'that it is not sufficient for you to say the boy is tough. How do you know? You said you didn't know him.'

'He has had to be, it seems. Very tough.'

'In what way?'

'In most ways, I should imagine. But I'd sooner you learned from someone else. I dislike repeating scandal.'

But Zoe makes him tell, all the same. Then the woman rejoins them.

'Well,' Jean says, 'do we all feel better for our good deeds?' She looks with cool eye upon Zoe and then looks out to sea. 'You'd think,' she observes, 'those two would tire of each other.'

Zoe notices that the woman trembles, slightly but distinctly. And wonders if she trembles herself so visibly. Then she remembers the Professor. She finally glimpses him some way apart from the crowd, still standing aloof. But he is, of course, looking out to sea with the rest.

Has he tried to touch? She has not seen.

'Is no longer my dolphin,' Frank Yakich is telling the newspaper reporter. 'You have come this time to wrong man. Is everyone's now.'

'Electric all through,' says the old woman, before she faints again in the arms of her friends.

'You wait and see,' says the fat honeymooner. 'I'll have another go at the bloody thing tomorrow.'

'But what,' asks his wife, 'do you think you're doing now?'

'Having another go at you,' he explains.

Out in the bay, the boy and the dolphin have parted.

The pub roars. The telephone exchange is busy. The amphibian plane flies the newspaper people back to the world. Gossipers gather thick around Miss Murch in the post office. Those who have seen everything distribute the day fairly among those who have seen little. 'And there it was,' recalls old Miss Murch in scratchy voice much used that afternoon, 'as large as life again.'

Zoe, unable to see just where the boy has gone, rejoins the

Professor. Tony walks home with Jean. Ben Blackwood sits to his typewriter, still breathless from his climb home, and contemplates his first sentence of conviction for months.

'I wish I could do more for you,' Zoe tells Professor Thomson. 'So much more.'

'I come here for quiet,' Tony tells Jean, 'and find a pious riot.'

'Walk?' says the old woman, quite giddy with the brandy which has now three times revived her. 'I can dance.'

'I seen the golphin come back again,' says the gleeful child. 'And I rid that golphin, on its big back, I did.'

'A story from classical times enacted again on this improbable Pacific beach,' types Ben Blackwood solemnly.

'There's bound to be hell to pay,' Harry Green predicts to his wife.

'Yes,' says the old man in the pub, 'I touched the bugger. He's solid, all right, as solid as I stand here.'

The Garland boy sits on a flank of Hau hill in the last of the light, still shivering slightly, though the chill of the water is gone.

FIFTEEN

Today Ben Blackwood is by far first on the beach.

He has just mailed a story, by way of experiment; and so feels free, after a sleepless though not unpleasant night, to walk the beach in early morning, before sunrise, and before anyone else is about. He has never had the place so entirely to himself before. The laundered sand is crisp, crackling underfoot, and the faintly moving air is a cool intoxicant. The hills stand taut in the sunrise. In repose, without fleck or fin, the sea is thinly glossed with the new light. He finds himself, once or twice, looking over his shoulder, perhaps unwilling to believe himself alone.

After a time he arrives at the south end of the beach, where rocks stream with kelp, and trees hang about with shoals of shining leaves. He turns for home, the slender curve of the beach ahead. He is still alone, quite distinctly. For he can see his footprints, all the way back, in precise and lonely line on the impeccable sand. It seems he has always known this place.

He tracks an equally precise line of prints homeward. He proposes to breakfast upon smoked oysters and to get some sleep while he can. He looks over his shoulder once more before he leaves the beach.

'Sooner or later people are going to get sick and tired of the damn thing,' Harry Green announces over breakfast. Harry, on the whole, always feels more optimistic in the morning. But he has cause to wonder if his wife, the addle-brained female, is really listening to what he says. As she moves about the kitchen, she keeps looking out an open window, toward the sea, in furtive fashion.

'Are you with me?' he shouts finally.

'What's that, Harry?' The woman is as deaf as a doormat.

'I said, are you with me?'

'Of course, Harry. I'm always with you. You know that.' And she peeks out the window again, possibly imagining he does not notice.

'I said the bloody thing can't last.'

'What thing, Harry?'

'This business.'

'Of course, Harry. Of course this business can't last. We closed it down two years ago.'

The bloody woman seems to think he is mental too.

'For God's sake,' he roars, 'this damn dolphin.'

'Harry,' she says vaguely, one eye out the window, 'I think there's enough excitement already. Without you adding to it.'

'Adding to it? Me?'

'You know what the doctor said.'

'Damn the bloody doctor,' he says. 'Damn the bloody dolphin.'

'I'm sure he means well, Harry.'

'Who?' he chokes. 'The doctor or the dolphin?'

'Well, both,' she says mildly. 'Both, I suppose. Now you mention it.'

'I mentioned no such bloody thing. Will you listen to what I'm saying?'

'You know I'm always listening, Harry dear.'

'I'm saying I mentioned no such bloody thing.'

'Then how can I listen to you, dear?'

'Of course you can damn well listen.'

'How can I listen to something you aren't saying? If you aren't saying anything, how can I possibly hear you? It really is most difficult.'

The woman is quite loopy with looking out the window. But Harry sees it would be uncharitable not to tolerate so lunatic a woman. He knows perfectly well no one else would. She has only him. It is always better, despite his inclination, to let the pitiful creature humour herself.

'Will you shut that thing?' is all he says finally, abandoning his bacon and gulping tea.

'What thing, Harry?'

Your mouth, he wishes to say. 'That damn window. It's blowing a draught.'

'Anyway,' she says thoughtfully, as she does so, 'I don't see why the business side of things should be getting you down again, Harry. It's all over. Harry, are you listening?'

But Harry, when she turns, appears to have gone to the garden. She opens the window again.

That day, perhaps the last distinct before time begins to stream, the first visitors arrive from the mainland, by boat and plane. Their newspapers have served the Motutangi dolphin again for breakfast entertainment, and this time they have to see. Most are ordinary enough sightseers, gently curious, neatly dressed, presenting no great demand.

Mr James Edward Farmer, 63, bachelor, retired, and one of the few adults to have so far touched the dolphin, declares his rheumatics gone. He hikes to the other side of the bay to pay his respects to Mrs Hazel Winter, the woman who yesterday shed her walking stick to general disbelief. Mrs Winter, who hasn't had a male visitor she can recall in five years, invites Mr Farmer to morning tea. Then he accompanies her to the beach.

It is the day that teachers at Te Hianinu school lose control of their children, those who have come, and those still remaining by midmorning.

It is also the day it becomes clear that the dolphin has, as they say, swallowed the anchor.

'Running low on ice cream and soft drinks,' says the sad-eyed storekeeper. 'We'd better lay in more, just in case.' He checks his shelves. 'And film too. We seem to have a run on that. We've just about cleaned out that stock we got two years back.' A thought appears to take him by surprise. 'You know,' he tells his wife, with a tremble of hope, 'we could do quite well out of this.'

'Then,' says his crisp wife, who has always had the better head for business, 'you'd better not go shutting down the shop today. If the thing comes back.'

That is plainly something he hasn't considered. 'You mean, stay here all the time?'

'That,' she agrees, 'is just what I mean.'

Zoe goes looking for the boy. She finds Tony ambling along the beach, with his wife. 'No,' he says, 'I've no idea where he lives. But he seems to spend a lot of time up on Hau hill.'

'Then perhaps he lives up there.'

Tony laughs.

'In some cave,' she suggests.

Again he laughs, as if she were not serious.

'For all we seem to know,' she adds.

'True.'

'I have often thought a cave might have its comfort,' she explains. 'From time to time. But I suppose that is not a terribly original idea. And it would be damp, besides.'

'And full of spiders,' Tony says amiably. He seems a pleasant man who likes entering in the spirit of things, though his wife is aloof.

'I don't know,' Zoe decides. 'They might be good company. There is probably more to them than you see, like sea-stars.'

'I know even less about sea-stars.'

'There is a great deal to learn. There are seventeen hundred known kinds. And possibly hundreds more never yet seen. Did you realize that?'

'Well, no.'

'There you are,' she sighs. 'The truth is quite exhausting.'

There is a pause. Tony's wife studies the tide.

'Are you sure,' he asks, 'that you really want to find the boy? After what I told you yesterday?'

'I think you're trying to frighten me,' she accuses.

'Not precisely.'

'Well, anyway, you needn't try.'

'No?'

'Because you couldn't frighten me any more than I am. I'm frightened enough.'

'I see. Well, don't say I didn't warn you.'

'The worst thing about fright, I find, is the difficulty breathing. And speaking.' Zoe pauses. 'And understanding what is said to you. For example, why am I ever likely to say you didn't warn me?'

'Because he's a tough customer. From personal experience, I can say you're unlikely to get very far with him, even if you do happen to find him.'

'Far? It is not a question of going far. Or going anywhere.'

'No?'

'No. It is just a question, so far as I see, of being here.'

'Then where,' asks Tony cheerfully, 'is your elderly friend this morning? Is he here still?'

'You could say that,' she says. 'You could say he is here too, in a way. But he is eating breakfast, at the moment.'

'That reminds me of mine.' Tony gives his wife a significant look. 'Perhaps we'll see you later.'

They walk off together. She hears Tony's wife saying something indistinct, and then laughing, as they move along the beach. Then she looks up at Hau hill. It looks big, and steep, and wild. And a long way from Professor Thomson over his breakfast. 'There's no need to wish you could do more for me, Zoe,' he said last night. 'And you mustn't think me ungrateful for what you have done, and tried to do, for me.' And, fixing his breakfast this morning, she has discovered there is also a limit to what she can do with his eggs. She even allows herself to wonder whether he tastes them.

David Garland is ready to leave the house early. Newspaper people were inquiring last night, and are likely to begin again this morning.

His parents do not know whether to be alarmed.

'They say,' says his mother, 'that you tamed this fish and brought it ashore for children to play.'

He cannot, after all, deny the substance of the thing. Though he can challenge detail.

'It took me along, to shore,' he says. 'And it was tame anyway. And a dolphin is not a fish.'

It is really all he has to say. But they persist.

'All this excitement,' his father says, 'do you think it's good for you?'

'There is no excitement,' he answers, 'and I will do what I like.'

This is undeniable. He leaves the breakfast table and goes out into the day.

His mood is milder by the time he takes up his look-out on Hau hill, the sweep of the bay below. He is not even much disturbed when the girl finds him there.

'I've been ages hunting for you,' she says, quite breathless. 'All over this hill.'

He is impressed, perhaps because it is obvious his parents would not have sent her, on any account. The sun is warm, and down in the bay people are scattered half the length of the shore.

She sits near him, on a split rock, and pushes back her hair, and her hat. 'I was told you hid up here,' she explains. 'After yesterday, I wanted to talk.'

'Well,' he says, 'go ahead, if you like. Talk.'

She appears to find this difficult. Anyway time passes.

'Go on,' he says.

'I seem to be having trouble,' she replies, 'getting back my breath. I'm not used to hills, you see.'

There is perhaps another minute of quiet.

'It is strange,' she remarks finally, 'that I had so many things to say, and that now I haven't. I am just as happy sitting here, saying nothing.'

They continue to sit, without problems. Looking down into the bay they can see Frank Yakich taking out his launch and cruising back and forward in the distance. He is obviously not fishing.

'You must forgive me,' she says, 'if I have nothing to say, after all. You must think it odd.'

'I'm not a great talker myself,' he confesses.

'I think what I wanted to say was about the dolphin,' she says, 'and your being friendly with it. But I have the feeling there is nothing to say.'

'You can just sit there,' he replies. 'I don't mind.'

'I think I might. For a while.'

It is difficult to tell who is most shy.

Presently he asks, 'You ever go fishing? Anything like that?'

'Not really.'

'I've seen you, sometimes, on the rocks. With an old man.'

'Not fishing. No.'

'I didn't think so.'

'It is hard to say what we were doing.'

'Then you don't have to say.'

'It's all right. It's just I thought he might help me with something.'

'And did he?'

'I suppose not.'

'Either he did or he didn't.'

'Then he didn't.'

'I go fishing sometimes,' he says. 'If you're interested. You don't have to talk much when you're fishing.'

'Anyway I get tired of talk,' she observes. 'There is never anything to touch or taste.' She pauses. 'It is pleasant just to sit here.'

Gulls drift high and quiet around the hill. They might have finished the morning there. But then Frank Yakich produces the dolphin, in the distance, and they scramble down the hill together, their hands at times becoming confused.

'I suppose,' says Tony, 'that we can make out as friends.'

'I wasn't asking for more,' Jean replies.

'It's in our nature to ask for more,' Tony says. 'And more.'

They arrive back on the beach a little late. The dolphin is already close inshore, with the boy and girl in control.

'Perhaps we're not needed,' Tony observes.

'Of course we are,' Jean says quickly.

The excitement is less than yesterday's, and there is no panic. Jean and Tony help clear space for the dolphin to move. When the children have finished, the adults begin to touch again. And the more people touch, the calmer the crowd grows. There are television cameramen darting.

Watching the dolphin from shore, Ben Blackwood speaks to an old man standing near.

'Who's that girl, do you know?' he asks.

'Girl?' says Professor Thomson, indifferent.

'That girl who seems to have adopted them both—the boy and the dolphin.'

'I'm a stranger here,' says Professor Thomson, who turns swiftly and walks away.

Ben is puzzled. He seems to have offended the man.

'If you like,' the boy says, 'you could swim with the dolphin too.'

'I tried yesterday. I can't swim far enough.'

'When I go out in the bay with it again,' he continues, 'I'll try to take it round the rocks, the other side of Hau headland. There are places there. The water's not deep. And there's no crowd.'

In the afternoon, after some hours away, the dolphin returns to Te Hianinu Bay alone. The absence of the boy, and the girl, is remarked; but not for long. For a child with sudden inspiration tosses his beach ball to the creature. The ball is nudged through the sea for some distance, then flipped high, to cheers from the shore. The dolphin does the same with a beer bottle, as encore.

Frank Yakich is trying, without much success, to locate able-bodied men who might, as vigilantes, protect the dolphin. The bay has always been short on able bodies.

Mr James Farmer and Mrs Hazel Winter are talking to the press.

Harry Green says he has always reckoned the island is the next worst thing to a lunatic asylum.

There are more people from the city. It seems summer has only just begun.

'I hope,' the child tells his sister, breathless, 'that golphin won't never go away now.'

SIXTEEN

The days begin a dance to the dolphin.

It has a name now. Motu, the children call it, then the newspapers. Motu, the Motutangi dolphin.

I'd like to be able to tell it all [*he writes*]. It's true I've become slightly more social. One can't altogether help it. Yesterday, Saturday, my storekeeper estimated two thousand trippers from the city or more. The guest houses are filled, the camping-ground too. The bay is bursting. So much for my peace. Still, this Motu has some character, and I confess to gawking with the rest. Sideshows have started to sprout along the shore, and this morning I saw a merry-go-round grown in the night. 'Not as good as Motu,' I heard one kid say as he clambered off a wooden horse. Business booms. Two stores actually on the seafront monopolize most of it. One to the north of the beach, the other to the south. If Motu spends too long to the north, business dies to the south, and vice versa. Motu, however, still has a plebeian dolphin weakness for the vibrations of an engine in the water. (One might have imagined by now that his pleasures were a little more recherché.) When his business began ailing one day, the north-end storekeeper took to the water in a dinghy, with his outboard motor on full throttle. He managed to guide Motu—and the crowds—in his direction, and his cash-register started tinkling again in most satisfying fashion. Comes massive retaliation. Next day south-end storekeeper takes to the water in dinghy with motor too, and fetches Motu to his end of the beach. Where his cash-register becomes musical. Their performance began to rival anything of Motu's. Yesterday, before a

151

vast audience, the battle of the storekeepers reached stalemate. Both took to the water at the same time, got Motu thoroughly confused, then crashed their dinghies. And sank. There were just these two heads bobbing about in the bay—they appeared still to be yelling at each other—and Motu weaving around in acute frustration. Who said Motutangi was dull? I wish I could tell it all. But I'm sure I couldn't do justice. As for these minor miracles you may have read about, well, there's not much to be said in one sense, though there is in another. I don't suppose we can afford to let poor Motu alone. Let Motu just be Motu, I mean. Yesterday I even saw a little girl dying of leukemia taken down into the water. She laughed, and perhaps that will remain miracle enough. But faith is a marvellous thing, and why not believe in Motu? (Indeed, why not? A chance for some new theologian, surely—not to speak of the fact that Christ was once symbolized by fish, into the melancholy bargain.) Of course you can't, perhaps, attribute everything to hysteria—all our minor miracles, I mean. I don't seem to be telling you anything about myself in this letter. Well, that may be accurate, in a way; maybe there's nothing to tell about myself. The faster I fade into the crowd, the faster I cease to exist. And even if it isn't in quite the way I expected, isn't this, after all, what I wanted? And all my little mysteries?—they cease, one by one, to exist too. No, there's nothing to say about myself. Nothing, in much abundance.

Jean rests on the sand beside Tony. 'What did this place do before?' she asks. 'Come to that, what did we do?'

Tony, face down in a towel, mumbles indistinctly. In any case Jean needs no reply. She looks out upon the serene sea. Like most islanders, she now finds her gaze always seaward.

'I said the sun's too warm,' Tony repeats.

'Too warm for what?'

'To make energetic use of memory.'

'Sloth,' she answers. 'The deadliest sin.'

'At least it makes the others insignificant.'

'Then it seems,' she says, 'I should aspire to your condition.'

'Be my guest.'

Jean looks down at Tony motionless on the sand. She can admire his lean and still interestingly youthful body without seeing any future in it. It does not, at the moment, even seem to possess much of a past. He could never be her victim; nor she his.

She has always found tomorrows difficult. Now she finds them inconceivable.

Her problem, after all, has never been with happiness; it seems a long time now since she believed in it, and now it rather astonishes her that any mature person can. It has, really, been with hope; and she sees it now as the most perverse, because self-inflicted, of all human ills. Perhaps, with hope shed, like a long fever, happiness could again be credible. Or peace at least, if she can find it in Tony's neutral company.

She discovers her gaze seaward again. 'Here it comes,' she announces, and looks at her watch. 'Motu's on time today.'

The fin has streaked from behind Hau headland and is zig-zagging across the bay. Tony shakes out of his doze. Likewise an elderly man, near by, lolling in a wheelchair. He speaks in wild babble to the young woman, possibly his daughter, attending him; his face has been damaged by a stroke.

'He's missing again,' Jean observes.

'Who?' Tony asks, quick on his feet.

'The boy.'

'Well, maybe he's found something more interesting—or someone.'

'What do you mean?'

'The girl's missing too. Little Zoe. My freckle-face girlfriend. Remember?'

'You're joking.'

'True. Surely you remember she went off looking for him, after the first day. The few times I've seen her, since then, she's always been with him. Or haven't you noticed?'

'Not always.'

'Then, darling, you have a remarkable blind spot. Are we going to fetch the fish?'

'You go ahead. I rather think I'm needed here.'

Tony races down to the sea and begins swimming toward Motu. Jean goes to the young woman who is struggling with the wheelchair. 'Can I help?' she asks. 'It's difficult, I know, in this sand.'

By the time Jean has assisted the perspiring and desperate young woman to shift the wheelchair down onto firm sand, Tony has brought Motu into shallow water. The wheel chair, moving with some momentum now, crashes into the sea, which rises over the legs of the groping invalid. 'It's all right, Dad,' the young woman says. 'We're nearly there.' To Jean she adds, 'He's been wanting this for days. But the excitement . . .' He is shivering and gasping with the shock of the water, and perhaps trying to say something. Jean gently guides the man's limp hand to the body of the dolphin; the fingers, suddenly trembling, make vain attempt to grip the stiff flesh. But the contact is made, nevertheless. And the old man smiles.

'I felt it,' he says, with surprising coherence, as he is borne back to shore.

There are other wheelchairs to come. They multiply daily. Wheels spin and stutter in the sand among the children. All along the beach people are entering the sea, their arms outstretched. A middle-aged woman in floral hat hoisting her skirt above bony knees; a pie-munching youth in jeans, trying to look indifferent; a man whose mountainous stomach spills an avalanche of flesh over the belt of his shorts; a timid young girl in her first bikini. Tony guides the dolphin among them, stroking and tickling by way of encouragement. Jean helps the children, and carries a big-eyed little boy with wasted legs. Tony, in his tight and narrow swimsuit, feels implausibly priest-like among the homage.

For he has begun to see hands, and hands alone. Lean long hands; hands fat and thick; graceful, quick hands; hands which seem all knuckle, and hands which seem boneless; hands without fingers; hands knotted into fists by arthritis; the searching hands of the blind; the gross, grabbing hands of the greedy. Hard hands and soft hands, hot hands and cool hands. Hands sure, and hands shy; hands gentle, and hands wild. There are hands he can love, hands he can loathe. And hands which leave him indifferent, though Tony is seldom indifferent now.

Harry Green is looking for his wife. The bloody woman was around the house only a few minutes ago.

'For Christ's sake,' he yells through the kitchen and then the hall of the Bella Vista, 'where the hell are you?'

The silence in reply is quite resonant. And lent some piquancy by the distant noise from the beach.

'I don't bloody believe it,' he tells the empty building. 'I just don't bloody believe it.'

But he has to, it seems. That bastard fish has stolen his wife.

At the end, Frank Yakich tosses Tony a rubber ball, and Tony punches it out to sea. Motu swerves after it, catches the ball on his nose, flips it back to his tail. The game is begun; after the homage, the circus.

Ashore, Jean is kneeling beside a child, and pointing. The child starts to smile.

A man in crisp white shirt and tie, who has arrived from the city too late to touch, attempts to swim out to the sporting dolphin and is suddenly bobbing, gasping, burbling in deep water. He cannot swim at all. Tony, trying to rescue him, receives a stunning clout on the jaw. But he can hardly expect gratitude from the cheated. He drags the man back to the beach and rests him on the sand. 'Never mind,' he says pleasantly. 'It's a lovely day tomorrow and the queue forms at eight sharp.'

At length Motu departs, leaving the bay awash with visitors and money. Tony and Jean walk home slowly. They pass Frank Yakich, with his ailing wife on his arm.

'Is another good enough day with our friend,' Frank observes.

Jean's hand engages with Tony's as they walk. There are other interruptions, questions, comments, from entire strangers along the beach. Friendliness, it seems, is an infection left by the dolphin's touch. The real miracle, for Tony. He is about to say this, when Jean speaks.

'I don't think one is alive,' she says, 'unless one is needed.'

A useful enough fiction to live by, he almost replies. As good as any other, so long as we prolong no illusion about our own need.

But her grip on his hand does not perceptibly tighten.

'And what about our friend?' he asks cheerfully.

'Our friend?'

'As Mr Yakich styles him. Motu. How would that apply? He's demonstrably alive.'

'He's needed. Obviously.'

'But what does he need? From us?'

They walk on a little further.

'I'm not sure,' Jean confesses finally. 'I hate to think.'

'Then try. If we're Nature's Frankenstein, as appears to be the case, mightn't Nature, in her collective wisdom, send a messenger?'

'A pretty capricious messenger. In a pretty random place.' Jean hesitates at the door of her shack, then unlatches the door. 'And why should she trouble with a messenger anyhow?'

'What would you do if you felt threatened, or abandoned?'

Jean laughs, shedding her swimsuit on the floor of the shack. 'Really, Tony. Don't go solemn on me. Threatened perhaps. But hardly abandoned. Or does she need regular reassurance?'

Tony shakes his head. 'I can see I'll have to think the argument out.'

'Well, let's reassure her for the moment, shall we?'

Making efficient love to Jean, on the floor and then the bed, Tony is overwhelmed by a vision of hands; they are all around him, claiming. Just as Jean is under and then above him, draining. Shuddering, he concedes his essence, yet is not released. Even this, he thinks, is not what was given us; it is what we have made it. In either denial or celebration, we make it other, as if it were ever important; or could be. In the act of sex, Tony at last finds himself celibate.

The hands recede. He sleeps. Jean, awoken, looks at the ceiling.

'These sea-eggs,' says Zoe, 'are quite pleasant and interesting to taste. If you don't mind the strong flavour of the sea, that is. I dare say, in time, I could work up quite an appetite for them.'

'Then try another,' offers the boy, still dripping from his long dive into the sea. He splits two more open on the rocks.

At his typewriter, Ben Blackwood tries to keep pace with demand. DELIGHTFUL MORE STILL, says his agent's latest cable.

PLEASE UPDATE ALSO CLARIFY OR EXPAND MIRACLES GLIMPSE NEW BOOK IN THIS DO YOU QUERY.

He seldom has time to get down to the beach now, or actually see the dolphin, he is so involved in telling about it. He even appears to be tiring of smoked oysters for supper every night. He feels at times he has taken out copyright on Motu, or at least become a public-relations man with unrivalled prospects.

DO YOU QUERY. He is having problems of focus with his eyes, let alone his mind.

For there seems no end to the things he is able to say, sentence locking with sentence, paragraph locking with paragraph. But sooner or later he hopes to find what he wants to say, not what he is able to say; he seems as far from that as when he began, for all the words. He suspects that if he dared lever up the words, unlock the sentences, then the paragraphs, he might find nothing within. Just a thin puff of smoke, perhaps, to show that something has perished.

Perished, that is, beneath such lines as he is typing now: 'While this little lost island, itself appendage of a little half-lost South Pacific country, begins to play host to visitors in mounting number, its star attraction—the tame wild dolphin, marvellous Motu—has been hastily protected by law. This has precedents here; two earlier wild dolphins from the open sea, said to have provided final vindication of Greek and Roman tales of dolphins and men, have been protected by specific law in New Zealand since the start of the century. Plagued by economic collapse, its agricultural produce in difficulty on the world market, the country already sees the dolphin as a possible godsend for its tourist industry. There is talk of building a large pool on the seafront to confine Motu and keep him on permanent show for visitors. Proponents of the pool point out that, despite the protection of law, the country's two earlier wild dolphins died in circumstances unknown. Critics of the proposal argue that the whole point about Motu is that he is unique in being wild and associating with humans of free choice; tame dolphins, trapped in pools, are to be found elsewhere in the world. Motu, they say, would no longer be unique. His pool, in effect, would be his memorial tomb. Fresh arguments blaze daily. In the meantime a token detachment of police has been sent to the island to control over-enthusiastic crowds and check vandalism.'

Ben Blackwood looks down the lines and changes a word or two.

That, decidedly, is not what he wants to say. So he writes another paragraph, still in search. And another.

YOU QUERY. He is definitely seeing double. He crumples the cable.

It turns out [*he continues*] that we have an author of sorts hidden away somewhere on the beach who, with his fluent journalese, has given Motu and Motutangi—and us—some unexpected if trifling international prominence. At least he hasn't spoiled a good story for want of telling it, shall we say. He's been pointed out to me by a storekeeper and I've since seen him once or twice fleetingly, prowling about the fringe of the crowds, earnestly asking questions. A rather shaggy and shapeless individual, seldom more than half-shaven, with bespectacled and bewildered face. I managed to find a book of his in the local library (open 2-4 Tuesdays and Thursdays, always provided now that Motu isn't performing). Pretty thin, wretchedly slick stuff. Efficiently time-killing. Though I put it down only a couple of days ago, I find it hard to recall just what it was on about, if anything. A pity Motu can't pick a better chronicler. No, I'm afraid he—our author, that is—doesn't make a new little mystery for me; nothing there at all. And certainly no mystery about why he churns out his present stuff—he's got a bigger monopoly than our two seafront storekeepers put together. No need for him to take to the water with an outboard motor. Or his typewriter; I doubt if its vibrations would impress Motu much anyway.

Professor Thomson, whose limbs have lately become as heavy as his dreams, is sitting at a sparse meal when Zoe appears. 'I came,' she announces, 'to see how you are getting on.'

'Nice of you to wonder,' he says. 'I don't seem to see you often now.'

She makes no comment. Instead she makes herself at home in his kitchen, with his teapot.

'I imagine,' Professor Thomson continues, 'that everyone is getting pretty weary of the fish by now.'

'Perhaps,' Zoe concedes. 'It may be true of some.'

'I tend to avoid the beach now,' he says. 'I imagine I might leave altogether, when I find the energy.'

'But why?' Zoe appears honestly startled.

'The crowds.' Such explanation seems unnecessary.

'They are happy crowds, mostly.'

'And the noise.'

'Mostly laughing. And sometimes singing, in the evenings, where people are camped. It can be pretty in the evening, where people are camped. All those tents glowing among the trees, like lanterns.'

'All the same,' he says.

'Perhaps it is the children crying,' she suggests. 'They laugh and they cry. Children are like that.'

He shakes his head.

'Or the drunks,' she goes on. 'I see people drunk, after the dolphin has been, though not often bad-tempered.'

'I just know it is not the same,' he insists.

'Of course it is not the same. I never said that.'

'But not the same for me.'

'That,' says Zoe, pouring tea for them both, 'is where you are wrong, at last. It is the same, for you.'

'I think I know my own life best.' He cannot imagine why he should be arguing, in so futile a fashion, with this scruffy little girl who takes liberties.

'It is the same, only worse,' she says. 'I doubt, for example, that you have ever really looked at children after they have touched the dolphin, and sat astride.'

'I have seen the crowds stampede.'

'If that is all, then you may as well see nothing.'

'And people making themselves absurd.'

'If you see nothing,' she says, 'how can you know anything? And how could I have thought it?'

There is a silence in which both retrieve themselves, where they can, and their tea grows cool.

'That is your affair,' he answers finally. 'I offered nothing.'

'If only . . .' She sighs.

'If only? Yes?'

'I should never say those two words; I promised myself once. My father said life could be made of if onlys.'

'Never mind your father.'

'If only you would try again to see what others cannot see. I think you did, once.'

'And I also told you, once, it was too late.'

Zoe for a moment appears to accept this. She sips tepid tea. Then she grows restless. She leaves her chair and wanders the cottage, picking objects up and putting them down, perhaps seeking illustration, or perhaps just something to end the long silence. At length she comes to the sea-star collection, each jar fastened down on a creature preserved and labelled, always meticulously named.

Plutonaster knoxi (abyssal star), she reads finally, in neat hand, on the jar she seeks. And she sees the orange-red of the star has faded to fawn; hardly a colour at all.

'So it is all for nothing,' she observes. 'And you'll go away.'

'The crowds,' he begins.

'I don't believe,' she says, 'that you have even touched the dolphin. Or tried.'

The inconceivable has to be conceived, though it is difficult for Zoe. Even when he does not contradict her.

'What for?' he asks. 'Another miracle? I think the island's already rather overburdened with those, don't you?'

He has grown unused to the sound of scorn in his own voice. To his surprise, Zoe weeps; she sits down in a chair and weeps. He does not know what to do, how to manage. He stands with unease beside her, fiddling with a large pocket handkerchief. In the end, since he must do something with it, he uses the handkerchief to polish his glasses.

'I'm sorry,' he says.

'You don't have to be sorry.' 'No?'

'No. You see, I'm not weeping for me.'

The crowds [*he adds*] appear to be getting younger. I don't mean in terms of children; they've always been around. At first they seemed, the crowds, made mainly of the very young and very old. Now we're getting those in between. The adults grow younger daily. These appalling mini-skirts everywhere and leggy creatures bouncing their busts to the sound of transistor radios. And lusty lads loping the length of the beach. Really. It's almost too much. At this very moment, I imagine, our Mr Blackwood (our author) will be making studious report on the swinging scene. That, surely, will be his fertile phrase.

Harry Green has known all along what it might come to. Perhaps not exactly; but more or less, near enough. First his foolish and faithless wife. Then more adequate advance warning in the pale shapes of copulating couples in the light of his torch when he stalks his beach frontage in late evening, warding off prowlers. If it happened once in a past summer it would have been once too often, but he has now, with his cries of agitation, flushed shamelessly tangled torsos from the trees three nights in succession. He sleeps, and dreams, uncomfortably. It may only be a matter of time before his garden itself is invaded, used furtively as park for promiscuous pleasures. Finally he loads a rifle and stands it by his door. And next day his worst fears materialize; they arrive long-haired and unkempt, with beards and shawls, bells and beads, from the city. Possibly, probably, just an advance guard.

'Love,' they chant. 'Love, love, love.'

SEVENTEEN

Within a half-dozen days the hippies are everywhere, and their flowers.
There is hardly a wheelchair without a garland. And girls swim out to
deck the dolphin. It sometimes seems awash with blooms.

'Yesterday,' types Ben Blackwood, 'fifty army men were dispatched
to reinforce the growing contingent of police here to keep the peace
of the island. Vice-squad members are reported checking out stories
of drugs and orgies. But so far there has been no real trouble. A
rumoured demonstration about the war in Vietnam proved only to be
a flowery protest against the threat to Motu's freedom of choice. For
it now appears inevitable that Motu will be made permanently captive
in a pool—he can still, it is said, be billed as the world's most unique
wild dolphin. The argument which seems to be winning the day in
official circles is that capital for exploitation of Motutangi as tourist
resort is unlikely to be forthcoming unless Motu's continued presence
is ensured. As for the hippies they are in fact making love, not war, on
the island—according to their already traditional slogan. And islanders
and other visitors have, in the holiday atmosphere, accepted them
agreeably enough, like Motu himself. This festival of life (as one or
two more articulate hippies style it) may have suffered a jolt, however,
with the visit this week of a U.S. Navy man, actually passing through
the country on official business, who made a break in his crowded
timetable to fly in and see Motu "just out of personal curiosity". But,
he added, the navy was keeping a close eye on dolphins. "They have
some interesting sonar equipment," he explained. He envisaged a time
when his navy might usefully employ dolphins like Motu to carry
torpedoes, perhaps even nuclear weapons underwater.'

He pauses a moment, sighs, finally types a brief postscript.

Sequel to the first reported miracles on the island. Mrs Hazel Winter, 66 (arthritis), and Mr James Farmer, 63 (rheumatism), have announced their intention to wed. "Just as soon as we can," Mr Farmer told me. "All thanks to Motu." The everlasting miracle?'

Drugged with detail, Ben then takes his messages of the night into the morning. It is only eight, but the pale shore of Te Hianinu is already shaded with crowds. No one attempts to count the thousands. He passes a hippie encampment where smoke rises and guitars strum. A bright little girl in dark tights, with hair swinging long, dances to greet him. 'Good morning, Mr Blackwood,' she sings. And fixes a fresh flower behind his ear.

'What's this for?' Ben asks.

'For you,' she laughs. 'For the dolphin's laureate. Who else?'

'I'm overwhelmed.' He makes mock bow to her curtsy. And receives a flirting kiss on his cheek before she darts away.

His unsteady step quickens on the way to the post office. Miss Murch, the postmistress, seems quite taken by his appearance.

'I see you've joined them, Mr Blackwood,' she declares. 'I see you've joined the flower people. Behind the left ear too.'

'An honorary posting,' Ben replies.

Frank Yakich goes out in his launch. Motu still keeps him company as of old. Which makes fishing difficult, and besides upsets the crowd ashore.

Eventually he cuts the engine, perhaps a mile out from the beach. In the silence Motu glides close alongside.

Frank gestures out towards the open sea. 'Why don't you,' he appeals, his eyes bleak, 'bugger off? Before is bloody too late?'

Motu rubs alongside the boat.

'Bloody thing,' Frank says with affection. 'Stupid bloody thing.'

He starts the engine for the run home. Motu leaps ahead.

Professor Thomson has resumed his private journal, for some reason. The last entry was shortly before his wife died. He has never felt able to make cold record of her death.

'Has it struck no one,' he writes, 'that the stories of friendship between man and creatures truly of the wild virtually cease with the advent of the Christian era?'

After some reflection, he inserts 'Western' before 'man'. But it does not help. Whatever he intended to say, and wants to say, remains unsaid.

His windows are shaded against the warmth of the sun, shut against the noise of the day.

'What else,' he adds, straining, 'may we conclude has been lost?'

He is attempting, he realizes now, to write some postscript to his stay on the island. If he can find it, sum up gracefully, gather in all the ends, he will feel free to leave.

'A sense of our now imprisoned animality?' he asks his journal. Then he deletes the sentence and begins again. 'Did man . . .'

No.

He rises, sets down his pen, crosses the room. At the window he draws apart the curtains, looks out on the day. There are people in immense number, and in preposterous variety, dawdling up and down the road, to and from the beach. He would give anything, he knows suddenly, to see the road empty again, and a girl in odd attire across the other side, thin book in hand, waiting.

Zoe. A name with the echo of a cry, the sound of a lost garden. If he has always been precise about names, it has evidently not been to forget.

Did I [*Tony writes*] call it a swinging scene? I should have said a carnal carnival.

There seems barely room on the beach for Jean and Tony this morning. It is difficult for them now to keep a grip on the place they remember, and other things.

They are no longer really needed. Motu, these days, threads his own way through the crowds. All pink legs appear equally friendly.

They are spectators again. The days drift; so do they. Tony examines a newspaper discarded on the sand near where they finally choose to sit. *Grubby Louts Said to Deface Country's New Tourist Centre,* he sees. *New Threat to Motu's Peace?*

He finds it a relief to know there is still a world beyond the beach, however perverse. A world where people are evidently capable of pronouncing judgements, making decisions.

But he does not say this to Jean. They no longer speak much. It seems they cling to each other in much the same way as they cling to their old part of the beach, among the growing mounds of ice-cream wrappers, out of habit. They are, both of them, back to waiting.

'Something's just struck me,' Jean says, out of somewhere beyond him. 'Have you noticed Motu always appears now from the south of the bay? At the beginning he always came from the north.'

'You have a keen sense of direction.'

'Always from behind Hau headland now,' she continues.

'Well?'

'It's just a thought.'

But, in the end, Tony decides it rather more.

Harry Green stands in his plundered and newly colourless garden. Last night, despite his torchlit wandering till late, it was stripped entirely. What price his sweat now, all his care, all his love? The hibiscus shrubs stand bereft of bloom. The rose bushes are ripped. The Japanese fuchsia is a wilderness of snapped stems. There is not a flower intact. Just a path of petals toward the shore.

This, Harry tells himself, is the bloody end.

He goes roaring to his telephone to call the Minister of Police person-to-person, collect.

'I love you,' says the intense long-haired young man.

'Yesterday you told her that. The same thing. I bet you did. I saw you with her.' The young woman is rather fierce.

'That,' he says, 'was yesterday.'

'And today you love me.'

'I do,' he agrees. 'I really do. I'm not ashamed to say it.'

'Oh well,' she sighs. 'I suppose today is better than nothing.'

'It always is,' he insists.

'And better than never at all.'

'And all we've ever got,' he finishes. 'Shall we,' he asks presently, 'wait to see if old Motu makes the scene today?'

'I saw him yesterday.'

'Of course,' he says. 'Yesterday.'

'I don't forget yesterday easily,' she observes.

'I didn't say you had to. Now it's up to me to make today more memorable.'

'And you really do love me?'

'Naturally. Didn't I just say so?'

'Then we won't wait for Motu. After all, what more can he give us today?'

'Now you're swinging,' he says.

Motu is sighted at eleven, a little later than usual, leaping into the bay from the south. People in dozens, then hundreds, race into the water, to wait, in case he should pass near.

Even the engineers, measuring out a possible pool for Motu, and testing for foundations, stop work to try their luck in the sea. And behind and among the crowd police and army men patrol in twos and threes.

'Come on,' Tony says finally. 'Let's go.'

For they have not stirred from their place on the sand.

'It's not our day,' he adds. 'It's no use hanging round.'

'Agreed.' Jean rises. 'But I wonder what's happened to him.'

'To who?'

'The boy.'

Tony shrugs. It is hardly the first time he has heard the question.

'We never see him at all now,' she observes. 'Less and less and now not at all.'

'Then he's like us. He can't take the beach any more. He's quit.'

'I expect so.'

'Like the girl. Zoe. We never see her either.'

They look at each other. Then they look south, for what it might be worth.

No, Tony would like to say; or protest. But of course he finds it impossible. 'So you wonder too,' Jean says.

'I can't see Motu,' says the child.

'Over there,' says his mother, still sweaty from their crowded trip.

'I only see people.'

'Among the people. See?'

'I just see people. All the people. Why are all the people?'

'For Motu. All the people are here for Motu.'

'I can't see.'

'Of course you can,' his mother snaps. 'The dark thing away over there. That's Motu.'

'I love Motu. I love his pictures in the paper.'

'Of course. And he loves you too. And that's him over there.'

'I love his pictures in the paper better. There aren't any people.' He pauses. 'If Motu loves me, then why won't he come to me?'

'You must,' his mother says, 'wait for Motu. Or wait for the people. And get used to disappointment.'

The old man nurses his wife over the dunes. They are almost at the beach.

'Sit and rest,' he tells her. 'We're nearly there.'

'All this way,' she says.

'It's been a long way,' he agrees.

'All this way,' she continues, 'and perhaps for nothing.'

'Won't you sit and rest?'

'Not now,' she says. 'After all this way. I can sit and rest any time. But I'll only ever see the dolphin once.'

'You're not going to die,' her husband insists with conviction.

'If you say so,' she says politely, to oblige him. 'But you'd better show me this one, just in case.'

He takes her arm again, and they descend the last few yards together.

The hippies serenade the dolphin among them. Flowers are flung, garlands hung. An extremely pale girl in the forefront, perhaps tubercular, certainly anaemic, rolls her eyes heavenward and faints in the sea, a streaming Ophelia among the flowers. Ben Blackwood, watching from his careful distance, has a brief pang of panic, then sees her lifted high, by four bearded young men, like a prone sacrifice, and borne gently back to shore. He returns to wondering how many more flowers the island can afford. The wonder is where they find them all. Surely song and love alone cannot account for blooms so many and bright.

'All you want is love,' a guitarist sings.

'Do you need anybody?' sings another. 'I need somebody to love. Could it be anybody? I need somebody to love.'

'With tangerine trees,' sings a third, 'and marmalade skies.'

Then, perhaps it is the sun, Ben is quite dizzy with the colour and sound, and he wishes all the flowers in the world could be enough, or all the love; and finally wishes wishing could make it so.

Yet he blunders blind into the sea, for the first time, to touch the dolphin.

EIGHTEEN

It is not a morning of promise. Under light cloud, the sea is unable to decide on its colour. Tony and Jean are on their way, early, along the headland under the rock outcrops, patchy pines and sheep-shaved slopes of Hau hill. The lingering chill of night makes their journey easier.

Tony is not happy. He is not sure, really, what they hope or want to find; and in any case he is less and less sure of his capacity to find anything. Ahead of him, Jean strides along with apparent certainties. They must now have travelled all of two miles along the rough going above the shore, though the distance from the bay is much less in straight line. Here and there, where they are obliged to travel low, the surge of a wilder, unsheltered sea flicks spray into their faces. They plunge through scrub, scramble over roots, brush through sturdy grasses.

They still have little to say. Soon Tony, with some relief, decides their quest futile.

'I can't,' he says, 'complain about lack of exercise today, at least.'

But Jean ignores him.

They climb a last lump of land, breathing hard, and look down on the end of the headland. Here the vigorous sea has shovelled sand between dark streamers of rock; the coast is broken into a multitude of bays, some tiny, some larger.

They can go no further, really. In its way a summary of all the journeys they have taken together, and returned empty-handed; except that this is literal and, almost beyond doubt for Tony, the last. He fails to see beyond the morning, just as he fails to see anything beyond this lump of land, apart from virgin bays disposed beneath, tangled with trees. The cloud is thinning now, and there are patches of brightness out to sea.

'Well—,' he begins.

But Jean grabs his arm, gestures him to silence. Then, above the sound of their breathing, and the beat of sea, he too hears the voices.

They travel quickly, quietly, in that direction. Until they are looking down, directly, into a narrow cove where the tide rises over the roots of shoreline trees and is sibilant among the rocks. Within this leafy frame of land the sea presently delivers into their sight three bodies. First the boy, then the dolphin, finally the girl.

They swim in line, the dolphin between. Then they dive, the three, with hardly a ripple. The sea colours; flashes of sunlight travel through the foliage above.

'See?' Jean says, unnecessarily; but makes no more of her triumph. She takes Tony's hand.

Together in the ambiguous morning, they watch the three bodies surface below, the pale girl, the brown boy, the dark dolphin. The girl is floundering now, weak in the water, and the boy goes to her help. The dolphin rides the slight swell, its tail moving lightly, and blowhole spouting.

Tony and Jean can hear the girl's laughter quite distinctly. Then the boy's. The steep chipped walls of the cove lend the sound a certain resonance.

'I didn't think . . .' the girl is heard to say, then the rest of the sentence is lost, together with the boy's reply. But their laughter is clear, and without ambiguity.

The sun is in Tony's eyes, or something; certainly he can feel the first warmth in the day, though that hardly explains why he seems so weakened.

The pair below shift out of sight, obscured by a tree.

Jean subsides slowly to the grass and Tony, linked, is obliged to follow. There is the smell of grass, the smell of sea. It isn't that Tony fails to see beyond the morning; he already, without much terror, knows the beyond. And Jean? Her breath is sharp in her throat.

'Look,' she says.

They are not the only bystanders. Professor Thomson has risen from the lip of a sharp slope, and stands trembling there. His eyes are wild, but they are evidently not for Tony and Jean. And it is plain that, from the angle at which he looks down into the cove, he can see much that they cannot.

Tony has a queer feeling of alarm. With his thin bony face, his dark suit, Professor Thomson appears less a presence than an apparition.

Laughter echoes up out of the cove again. And the apparition has to clutch his hat against the morning breeze.

Zoe tastes the boy against her as he helps her back to shore. It is the taste of trees and rocks, sand and salt, sun and rain. She would taste more, if she could, and is trying.

For the boy is tasting too, if that is what it is. He has only once seen eyes so bright.

The dolphin glides out of the cove. Professor Thomson backs away.

NINETEEN

Within a few days [*types Ben Blackwood*] the marvellous Motu, the wild dolphin of Motutangi, will be no more. Inside a week he should be just another of the world's tame dolphins, confined at first in a temporary pool, and later in a larger and more expensive construction. Perhaps the last word in these accounts should be left to Plutarch, who observed that the dolphin was the only creature who loves man for his own sake, 'though it has no need of any man'.

His final spurt of borrowed eloquence leaves him feeling faintly drunk; he has told everything and said nothing. Perhaps he cannot have his story and live it too. Or perhaps he can blame those among whom he has fallen. For last night his drunkenness, on bad red wine, was more literal; his cottage seemed to balloon with the pressure of people and hover high above the island. Around him, in pleasing daze, he heard of love and—well, love again. But when they left, truth sat solid as stone in his stomach. He sees his problem, after all, has never been with belief; it has been with believers.

Anyway he finishes the last sentence of the last paragraph, and knows it time to quit. He supposes truth need not always be fatal, if diagnosed in time. He has only to begin again.

He takes the last of his morning strolls towards the post office, and the amiable Miss Murch. But there appears to be some uproar along the way. Around a clump of vegetation, beginning to step carefully, he comes upon hippies tangling with the police again. He sees banners rise and fall, SAVE OUR DOLPHIN and MOTU FOR KING and ALL THE WAY WITH LOVE, and flowers thrown high. Then, though he cannot quite believe it, there are people falling; he sees truncheons flail. A handcuffed boy is kicked into a car. A mini-skirted girl on the ground is holding her head and screaming. Another boy is endeavouring to examine the blood which leaks spectacularly from his split head. There may be more for Ben to see, but the crowd, and the violence, licks round him; and he finds himself at the centre, making absurdly precise protest. There are the buttons of a police uniform directly before him, and a young clean face, more indifferent than brutal; but the truncheon swings down all the same. At least, Ben thinks with some relief before the detonation, I can damn well believe in you.

The excitement ebbs before noon, and in any case Motu is on time again. With the hippies pruned, banners broken and burned, and the beach that much tidier, workmen proceed with the temporary pool.

Professor Thomson, his heart quick, walks the rocks alone that evening. Motu has left the beach, but perhaps not the bay. Kelp rises upon the sunken tide; perhaps starfish too. But his obstinate eyes will accept only a fin, if they can. As dark takes the world's sharp edges he sees, at last, what seems the dolphin glide close to the rocks, a few feet away, and knows his chance as near as ever it will be; the creature is evidently pursuing small fish into the shallows. Without pausing to strip shoes or jacket, he jumps into the sea; the water is over his head, and it is an unexpected effort to keep afloat. Among the streaming weed he recognizes, with prick of panic, that he is quite out of his element. The sound of sea is all around and perhaps the sound of other things too, like wilder music far away. The fin does not escape, as he thought it might; it veers straight towards him. He strains a hand to touch and then, sinking, extends both arms as in an embrace, to save himself from drowning. So it happens that those extremities of his body are first to be hit by the slashing teeth of the shark.

It is the third evening Harry Green has sat above the rocks, under the sunset. It is the third evening he has watched the surface of the sea, his rifle cradled. For he has heard the dolphin has been seen feeding near, and he is ready to wait.

Soon there is very little to be seen; land and sea begin to merge in the dying light. Stars appear and quickly brighten. The departed tide leaves rocks which could be fins, with dim flashes of foam.

At length he sees something which appears to move independently of the tide, of land or sea or sky—or is it his imagination? Anyway something afloat, bulking darker in the growing dark. His safety catch is off already; there is no point in trying for accurate sight. He fires once, twice, three times. He cannot see a thing now, really. He finishes emptying his clip of ammunition into the sea. It is his third clip; one for each evening. Sooner or later, he thinks, I am bound to hit the bastard. It stands to reason.

'We said friends,' Tony tells her. 'Not more.'

'True,' Jean agrees.

'You've got to have something to burn, to make a fire. I'm sorry, but there it is.'

'I'm sorry too,' she says calmly.

At the end of his outburst, he leaves in silence. Jean goes to bed alone and cannot sleep, though she expects his return in the morning. He has always returned before.

It really was [*he writes*] most intriguing to hear from you after all this time. You say I leave a lot of things unexplained. Perhaps true. What things most interest you? My little mysteries? They're so far in the past now I find them hard to recall. They sorted themselves out. Revelation, after all, need not be saved for the third act. What I mean is, life doesn't have third acts anyway. All things considered, two are quite enough for me. I notice you don't ask if and when I'm coming back again; in fact you make such a point of not asking there seems nothing else in your letter. Yes, if you must know, I have had a friend here. No, not the boy, as you suggest. You seem, one way and another, determined to misunderstand me.

Ben Blackwood, his head bandaged and dully aching, takes himself up the high winding track to his home in the dark. He pauses for breath, looks back on the bay. It seems, from hills to shore, a lake of lights. It is still difficult to accept, but then he cannot quite accept his day either. He cleared himself with the police finally, since his hair is cut reasonably short, and the growth on his face no more than one day old, but he finished standing bail for a dozen of his more hirsute acquaintances. If they fail to reappear in court, and he has no intention of ensuring that they do, then most of his summer earnings will be gone; the earnings which might have purchased him an escape. He does not, however, find himself much distressed. The money Motu brought has never seemed very real anyway.

He arrives at his door, which is for a moment unfamiliar, because of the chalked slogans. LUV, says the one at the top. BEN BLACKWOOD'S HOME AWAY FROM HOME, says the one beneath.

He opens his door and meets the scent of crushed flowers and the sight of a refugee camp. There are bodies everywhere, variously and often immodestly disposed. Cans of food, opened and half eaten, clutter the floor; it appears his stock of smoked oysters has been cleaned out. A toppled flagon of red wine drips into a drying pool. There is a guitar or two, and bloodied bandages; a record-player, its batteries run down, spins sadly on the one cracked phrase of music. Most of the people are unconscious, scattered in attitudes of exhaustion or shapes of love. And it turns out that most of those technically conscious have tripped elsewhere. A young man half-rises to greet Ben, eyes glazed, and falls back again.

'We have to,' he says, articulating with effort, 'do something about tomorrow.'

'True,' Ben says. 'Unless tomorrow's already done something about us.'

'Another day or two,' the young man gasps, 'and they'll have that pool finished.'

'Very likely,' Ben agrees: and passes on.

His bed, he finds, is occupied by two tumbled girls; he will find no rest there. So he turns back to his desk of door and boxes, which rises rather monumentally among the fallen, and sits down to it, for lack of any other situation. He rolls a sheet of paper into his typewriter and lights a cigarette, cautiously, to see what will happen.

'Tomorrow?' he types. 'No more than a quick peeling away of possibilities, a slow erosion of probabilities. And then it is as naked as yesterday. And as obstinate.'

To his surprise, with a rush of clicking keys, or perhaps chinking chains, something does begin to happen.

Tomorrow?

TWENTY

The dolphin rests in the cove, on sand near the high-tide mark, some way out of the sea.

The boy, just after dawn, is first to find it. The morning has the cool which comes towards the end of summer, and he has dressed more warmly than usual for his tramp the length of the headland. For weeks now he hasn't cared to squander an hour of daylight beyond the cove; food plundered from the family kitchen swings from the pack on his shoulder, enough for Zoe and himself to last the day. By the time Zoe herself arrives, he will have cooked their breakfast, as has been his habit, on the rocks above the shore, and perhaps caught a fish or two for lunch. He would find it hard to explain how the days so swiftly vanish. Conversation seldom troubles them, and people never. He doesn't have to think much about Zoe. She is simply there, and it is sufficient that she should be. Imagination hasn't suggested a time when she should not.

For there hasn't been much, really, which Zoe hasn't seemed to understand. Even the dare game, and its consequence.

'I think I would have liked that game myself,' she confided. 'Though I have never been very good at climbing cliffs. People taught me other things, sometimes things I would sooner not have learned. I would have been better off with cliffs, I mean, or most things else.'

He has grown used to the strange things she says, and sometimes laughs. Anyway they are, one way and another, careful not to let talk become too much a habit, while there are other things. At times he finds it difficult to believe there is anything beyond the cove, or could be. It is quite as difficult as recalling the time before the dolphin, though he still tries that now and then.

She has had things to learn. How to throw a line, or thread a sinker. How to cook mussels, or eat sea-eggs. How to swim without effort, and dive down to the deep green weed with the dolphin.

The cove itself is a shell which they fill; he likes to take it by surprise in the mornings, to see it empty, to see it nothing but rocks and trees and sea, to see it before Zoe and Motu and himself weave through the water. For days can still surprise: there are no two alike. There is always something new with Motu, new with Zoe; it is hard to distinguish between, even if he tries.

That day, though, offers more than morning, and less. He sights Motu from high, and begins to run. His legs, on the slope, seem never to connect with the ground; he is beside the dolphin within seconds. The blood has grown sticky on its flanks, around the places where the shark has ripped. He sees that the creature still lives, if just. The breath from the blowhole is warm; there seems a chance to save it, if he can get it back to the water.

The clown's smile, though, appears sad. There is a faint, drawn-out squeaking sound.

He tugs at a flipper, then at a tail-fluke. He moves the creature, all right, but deeper into the sand and only little nearer the tide.

Then he sees the dark skin is dry, and will soon burn under the sun. He strips his clothing, piece by piece, and drenches it in the sea; and covers the creature as much as he can, which isn't much. In doing this, he finds the original wound, and understands. It was apparently not enough to kill, but enough to weaken. And blood and weakness drew the shark. He understands too, the same instant, that he is likely to be given credit for the wound, having already proved himself efficient with a gun.

In anguish now, as if admitting himself responsible, he puts a shoulder against an untorn flank and tries to heave. Again the dolphin shifts slightly, again deeper into the sand. It is heavier and far larger than he ever thought. The grace has become sheer bulk, barely yielding to his pressure, where once it danced to his touch.

The creature, in fact, hardly seems to be Motu at all.

Yet he has to save it, if he can.

His arms embrace its head, in familiar gesture. He hopes, with one sharp movement, to roll the body free of the sand. But he fails again, and falls, having opened at least one dry wound. The clothes which deck the dolphin blacken with blood, here and there.

He gathers them, takes them to the sea again, returns them sopping to Motu's skin. He places his hand to the blowhole. There is still warm issue of air. He hasn't failed entirely. Though life itself, survival, hardly counts as success.

He pushes, he pulls, he twists, he heaves. Sweat begins to blind him. And the dolphin is still only inches nearer the tide, when it needs to be feet nearer for life. It seems to become bulkier, heavier, by the minute. There is hardly a muscle in his body which does not ache. His feet begin slipping, skidding, in the sand, as his strength leaks away. And in the end he appears as near dead as the dolphin; he collapses, his heart a hammer.

Jean, arriving at the cove, finds the crazily garbed dolphin on the sand, and the naked boy weeping with frustration beside it.

Towards the end of night she found herself unable to wait for Tony. And with morning light she was walking out along the headland, following their route of yesterday. Her hope, if she had one, was perhaps that she might find Motu alone in the cove, and spend an hour there, doubtless her last chance before she leaves the island. For she cannot imagine herself much longer here, or Tony.

So she comes to the cove.

It is clear, at first sight, that nothing can be done for the dolphin. She bends to the boy; he jerks, and spins wide-eyed to her touch.

'You've got to help,' he says.

He takes her arrival for granted, in his urgency.

'But—'

'It's got a chance,' he says, 'in the sea. We've got to get it back in the sea.'

His nakedness seems to lend emphasis. His tears, unless she imagined them, are already dry.

'Please,' he says. 'You've got to.'

As if she wouldn't.

'Of course I'll help.'

Together they struggle with the creature, now deep in the sand.

And, one way and another, joining their strength, move it foot by foot toward the water. As they shift it, the boy's bloody clothes fall from the dolphin's back, leaving its injury naked. All reason for hope should be gone. But Jean finds herself hoping.

It has to live. It must.

They reach the sea, despite the clinging shore, and begin edging Motu into the water.

'This way,' the boy instructs. 'That way. That's it.'

Now the dolphin is afloat, or nearly, and reacting to the water. The boy tries to steer it further; and finds difficulty.

'It keeps pushing back,' he cries with dismay. 'Back to shore.'

Then, with a heavy lash of its tail, the dolphin is half back on the sand again.

'They do that,' Jean observes, exhausted and breathing hard, 'or so I've read. They come ashore to die.'

'Then we have to fight it,' the boy announces. 'And keep it in the sea.'

He begins to push again, so it seems she must too. But it is like a battle with a falling wall. The dolphin, despite its diminished strength, knocks them both aside as it crashes back on the shore.

'You see,' Jean says, 'it's made the choice. The only thing we can do is let it die.'

But the boy isn't listening. He is trying to drag it back in the water, by the tail.

'Leave it,' she pleads.

He doesn't answer. By himself, he may have shifted it an inch or two.

'Leave it,' Jean cries. 'Let it die.'

Perhaps he has moved it another inch.

'You must,' she adds. 'We must.'

He falls down in the water, rises, begins to tug the tail again. He seems to have forgotten her. And seems drunk with his effort, falling, rising. He begins beating his fists against the dolphin, as if to awaken it. And then tugging again. Jean has never seen such fury. She stands paralysed, powerless. She has become irrelevant again, it appears, familiar to herself.

'Please die,' she says, perhaps to the dolphin.

For it has to have an end. The boy seems quite manic now. And the dolphin is a dying, ugly lump of flesh. But of the two the boy, with his demented energy, is by far the more terrible. And threatening. Like a boulder begun rolling; and Jean has to stay clear of his path, or make it easier. Yet she is surprised how cool she is, how free. As if purged, exorcized.

He appears determined to tear the dolphin apart, to breathe life into it again. Anyway his fingers are scrabbling along the flesh of its back, seeking purchase. Finally he falls, despairing, across Motu, and then begins sliding away, collapsing into the sea.

Two walkers, having loved till late, find what is left of Professor Thomson that morning, cast up on the sand of Te Hianinu Bay. They draw a crowd swiftly; a crowd which, unlike those of days past, grows quiet at its centre. And the quietness spreads. It is a shifting crowd, with most people walking quickly away.

Tony, out on the beach early and going nowhere in particular, though he expects he may finish up breakfasting with Jean, is one of the people drawn. He needs only the one look, and backs away. He recognizes the dark suit, but not much else. There isn't much else to recognize.

He notices how noisy feet are, on the sand; a restless scratching. He sees sky, water, faces. He also overhears fragments of human speech. He is still trying to compress the details, lest they fly apart even further, when Zoe rises into his sight. She is clearly on her way somewhere, with small kitbag over her shoulder.

'What is it?' she asks him.

For there are legs obscuring her view.

'Never mind,' he says, trying to steer her around. 'Don't look. Just walk away.'

But she isn't so simply persuaded. She holds her ground, obstinate. 'Why shouldn't I look?' she demands.

'Because it's someone you know,' he says. 'Or knew.'

'Someone I knew?'

'The old man. He—'

Before he can finish, she flashes away into the centre of the crowd.

'Anyone know him?' a voice asks. The question has possibly been asked several times; it is the first time Tony hears it.

Still ineffectual on the periphery of the crowd, he is about to reply himself, when he hears Zoe's voice in the centre. 'Yes,' she says quietly. 'I know him very well. Very well indeed.'

The doctor arrives, and the ambulance, and when the body is taken the beach horror shrinks to beach sensation. Tony guides Zoe away, through the dispersing crowd, toward his cottage. Her distress has begun to show.

'He looked,' she recalls, 'something like my father.'

For a moment Tony is confused. 'Old?' he offers.

'No,' she says. 'Dead.'

Jean, with relief, at last sees what she can do. She goes to the boy. The tide is around his chest, and his face barely clear of the water. He will have to give in now, or drown.

'Come on,' she says. 'There's no more to be done.' She tries to grip him, drag him clear. But he changes swiftly from a limp weight, as if she has tripped some inner spring.

At least he is aware of her again; he strikes her down. She swallows water. Then he strikes her down again. She swallows more water, and swerves clear of his rage.

She finds her own fury. She escapes the water and, looking about wildly, sights a rock. Then, lifting it with two hands, she slams it down on the skull of the beached dolphin. Again and again, until she is sure of death.

It is all over. She sees the boy is quite finished too, virtually helpless in the sea. She brings him ashore; he has no resistance at all. He appears reasonably intact, though there is a choking sound in his throat as she rests him on the sand, in the shade of a rock, clear of the tide, still quite pliant. She nurses him there. All the awkwardness and anger is gone. It is difficult to believe he frightened her.

'It's all right now,' she says. 'There was nothing we could do.'

He doesn't stir. Perhaps he hears.

'You'll find,' she goes on, 'other things. So this won't seem important. After all, you're still alive.' She tries to believe this and, with effort, almost does.

He begins to shiver. It is still a cool morning, despite the sun, and his sweat is drying slowly with the sea on his cold body. His bloody clothes, strewn upon the beach, promise no warmth. So Jean takes off her jacket and works it around his shoulders.

'There,' she says, though the cover is inadequate. 'That better?'

Still no response. But at least his shivering confirms life. She is content to wait. And, after some time, he does speak. His level voice surprises.

'What are you doing here?' he asks.

She is quiet a moment. 'Like you,' she says finally, 'I came to swim with Motu.'

'But how did you know about this place? Did Zoe send you?'

'Zoe?'

'She must have. Only Zoe and I knew about this place. We've had it to ourselves.'

'I know.'

'Then she told you everything. Why did she send you? And why isn't she here?'

'Don't upset yourself again. You've had enough for one morning. Let's just say I happen to be here. And I don't know where Zoe is.'

'Then she's gone. That's it. She's gone and told you to come instead. Well, never mind. I don't care. It's all over, all finished. I don't care any more. And it's just too bad about you, coming so late.'

He rises and stalks away from her, with all the dignity he can summon on naked legs, and picks up his scattered clothes. He flings back her jacket: it falls short, between them on the sand. And he begins dressing. The sight of the dolphin, turning belly upwards on the tide, halts him for a moment; but only for a moment.

'Well, that's it,' he observes. 'It doesn't look up to much now, does it?'

Jean can no longer imagine the weeping boy she found. Dressed, he seems to have a brutal strut, as if he has found the fit of his shell.

'There's nothing left here,' he adds. 'See for yourself. Or was there something else you came for?'

'No,' she says finally.

'Well,' the boy announces, 'please yourself.'

With his slight swagger, he leaves the cove. After a time, still tired, Jean does too. She looks back on the place once. It is empty and quiet. The carcass of the dolphin rocks on the risen tide.

Tony feeds the girl brandy. Her eyes, however, remain unreasonably wide and entirely beyond him. He scatters words liberally into the silence around her. She makes no real response, though she is evidently prepared to drink all the brandy he can pour. When she does speak finally, it is with unexpected precision; she rises with the words and sets down her glass.

'I recall,' she says, 'that I have an appointment to keep this morning.'

Her precision, however, goes no further than her words. She wobbles.

'Can I help?' Tony offers.

She considers this. 'I dare say,' she says. 'I dare say you can.' She takes a swaying step either towards him or away from him, an entirely ambiguous motion; he catches at her arm as she drifts. 'My feet,' she adds, 'seem a problem, among other things.'

Tony, having needed brandy himself, is not the ideal escort. They swerve to the door together, where they collide.

'If you could,' she continues, 'come with me some of the way at least, I would be grateful. Then I would not be alone, would I?'

'You would not,' he agrees.

'But what about your wife, where is she?'

'I haven't a wife. Perhaps you mistook someone.' Tony pauses. 'Excuse me,' he says finally, leaving Zoe propped against the door, and returning inside to fetch the brandy. He thrusts the bottle in the back pocket of his trousers, where it bulges.

He reaches the door again, though the floor seems tilted.

'I often mistake people,' Zoe says sadly. She fastens a hand on his arm. 'It seems my habit.'

'Oh?'

'Though I could not have mistaken him, this morning, could I?'

Tony is unsure what answer he should make. 'Try to forget it,' he advises.

'Why? It is better to remember him this morning, really.'

'Better?'

'Because it doesn't hurt so much.'

Tony cannot cope, that is clear. And the morning is perhaps worse, as they step clumsily out the door, into the sun again. Everything is formless and dancing—trees, sky, hills, water—in melancholy confusion. Even the track to the beach develops some surprising turns, as they lurch. Then there is the sand, which seems determined to trip, and the headland on to which they grope. It appears to be a place dense with edges, ready to cut and bruise, and scrape. Zoe is first to fall. She vanishes from his side quite suddenly, with a rattle of stones. Then he sees her some way down from the thin track, saved from the sea by the scrap of scrub to which she clings. She hangs there, quiet and rather expressionless, while Tony clambers down for rescue. At giddy length they both regain the track, and her grip on his arm is even more impressive. He wishes either that he'd had less brandy or had more; and then remembers the bottle in his pocket. He uncaps it, drinks, and shares the rest with Zoe. And they proceed. Their falls become more frequent but, in the long run, less painful. After a time, in fact, the landscape begins to float past steadily, even the sharp things of the headland. The world seems awash with revelation. Light leaps from the sea; the immaculate sky is huge. Green things eddy and trickle around them, in thick burst or thin frond, among the rocks. It seems the headland may march out into the ocean for ever. Then the landscape settles, as they breathe up the last few feet of rise, and look down into the cove itself.

It appears all has been preliminary; the scene could not be sharper, the forms more precise. They see the dead dolphin. They see the woman bending to the naked boy.

They may see other things too, though it is not the time to exchange. Zoe does not offer the slightest sound.

'Never mind,' he says. 'Don't look. Just walk away.'

They turn. At least he turns; and steers Zoe.

TWENTY-ONE

Just another fairy tale, Ben Blackwood sees with diminishing dismay; it is to be just another fairy tale after all. At least, he consoles himself cautiously, we may still need those. But he can still wish himself wholly convinced. After a while the click of his typewriter keys grows less steady.

He falls asleep, with daylight outside.

Motu is not seen that day, though a watch is kept. Frank Yakich goes searching in his boat, and brings nothing back.

Few people enter the water. It is not the chill of the sea.

'Where will you go?' Zoe asks. 'What will you do?'

'It would be more to the point,' Tony replies, 'if I asked those questions of you. I imagine I'll go back to where I used to live, with a friend, and find out if there's still a place for me there. If not, then I'll find somewhere else, sooner or later.'

'Then you aren't sure exactly?'

'Not even inexactly.'

She is silent for a minute. 'Then I wonder,' she says quietly, 'if I could come along with you, some of the way?'

Tony, for some reason, is not altogether taken by surprise. 'I don't see why not,' he says finally. Then something unnerves him. 'Is that what you did with the Professor?' he asks. 'Go some of the way with him?'

'I suppose that was it. As far as I could go.'

'Suppose I told you I knew where I was going?'

'Then I don't suppose I could come, any of the way,' she says. 'Could I?'

Tony leaves off packing for a while, and sits with his head in his hands.

Motu is not seen the next day either. Frank Yakich again goes in search, with no result. That night there are empty campsites, and few newcomers from the city.

'Is there something you want to tell us, David?' Mrs Garland asks.

For she has, after all, washed blood from his clothes. And he no longer spends his time outdoors. But he has not spoken of any hurt, or wound.

'No,' he says. 'Everything's all right.'

'You sure?'

'Perfectly sure.'

'Anyway,' she says, 'you've been looking much better for this summer, whatever you've done with it. I expect you'll have to be thinking about your future soon.'

'Yes,' he agrees mildly. 'I expect I will.'

On the third day it is conceded that Motu is gone. That day some people begin to speak of the strangeness of the thing, the appearance of a shark victim the morning of the dolphin's disappearance.

Harry Green emerges from his house and begins to walk his reviving garden, feeling it safe again. His sleep is better too; at least he has more of it.

The weather is holding. It looks like a long summer. Ripened paw-paws thud down upon his lawn; the banana trees unfurl new fronds with leisurely elegance.

'I hear,' he tells his wife, 'that Haze Winter has told silly old Jim Farmer just what he can do with his engagement ring. She says she's not up to his high jinks, not at her age.'

His wife appears to be listening.

'It's good to know,' he observes, 'that some people don't lose their heads.'

On the fourth day, the day after the inquest, speculation becomes legend. For the more mystical, having bided their time, say Motu has returned himself to shore in original human form. He never was, they say. Even Frank Yakich, a realist of the sea, is quiet for lack of better explanation.

The workmen have abandoned the beach. Small waves snap about the piles of their unfinished pool. And the police have almost entirely retired to the mainland.

Guest houses have vacancy signs.

'Where,' asks the child, 'has golphin gone?'

'The dolphin,' replies his sister, 'has gone far away, over the sea.'

'Will golphin come back again?'

'Perhaps, if we wish,' says his sister. 'If we wish hard enough.'

'Then I will wish,' declares the child. 'I will wish hard. I will wish till I burst.'

His tall sister leans into the breeze and looks out to sea.

'I will wish too,' she says.

On the fifth day, the day after the funeral, Frank Yakich goes fishing again. Harry Green wishes to hell his wife would stop weeping.

The surviving hippies leave the island, flinging the last of their faded flowers upon sea and shore.

'Motu lives,' one calls, and the cry is taken up. 'Motu lives.'

It is dusk as they dance their way along the sand. There are guitars and bells and pattering drums.

Jean, who has been walking the shore alone, finds herself among them. A youngish man grins and grabs her, whirls her in a dance. In the end she is quite breathless, though she can still manage to laugh.

'See?' he says. 'You flip. You're really one of us.'

'Not today, thank you,' she replies politely.

'Don't lose your cool,' he insists. 'Remember what that crazy dolphin told us. Remember what old Motu came to say.'

'And what's that?'

'We haven't got anything but love, baby.'

'Well, it's better than nothing, I admit.'

'What did I say? You make the scene, old sister.'

Finally she falls, limp and lost, against the side of a sandhill. She sees, when she finds her breath, that she is not alone there. A bespectacled man, faintly owlish, is lighting his pipe, and watching the hippies depart. His face, seen in the flickering flare of his match, is serene and perhaps strong. And his smile is interesting, up to a point. She has noticed him once or twice, before the crowds. He seems another survivor of the summer.

'Well,' Ben Blackwood hears a voice beside him say, 'and what do you think?'

It appears he is not left lonely after all.

'What do I think about what?' he queries gently.

'About them. About anything. Or everything.'

He shrugs.

'You must think something,' she protests.

'Now and then,' he admits.

'Well, go on. For example, since the point has just been raised, what do you think our dolphin was on about?'

He is slow to make an answer.

'Innocence?' she offers.

'If that was all,' he begins.

'Yes?'

'Then it was wise to pack it in,' he says. 'We have to make do with ourselves.'

She seems, from her silence, disappointed.

'Never mind,' he finishes. 'If we don't deserve Moby Dick, then why not Mickey Mouse?'

Scraps of music, blown back along the shore, reach them in faint gusts; the last of the hippies bounce and bound away into the dusk. Soon there is only the sound of the advancing tide. The frothy edge of the sea is a luminous line.

'And that's all?' she asks. 'All you think?'

'Since you ask.'

'Well, I can't say it's news to me. Of course we have to make do with ourselves. You're not telling me anything. Anything, that is, I don't really know.'

'That,' he says, 'is possibly the point.' He rises slowly and dusts sand from the seat of his trousers. 'Can I,' he adds, 'invite you home for a drink?'

The beach seems distinctly different. Possibly it is just that he is not alone. They walk together over the sand, following the curve of the shore, the other way from the hippies.

On the sixth day it is clear all the outsiders have gone. Motutangi is back in season.

An old couple, pensioners, have the beach almost to themselves on their morning walk. Their elderly dog, its hair grown patchy, waddles behind. Now and then it stops and scuffs among lingering litter. And now and then the old couple stop and stand quite still, leaning on their sticks, looking out to sea.

On the seventh day Frank Yakich is fishing. The brown hills of Motutangi, like the spine of a long lizard, stand sharp in the sun. He is glad to escape the shore, though the fishing is indifferent and hardly worth his while.

He pulls in his nets for the last time. He has not expected much, so is not disappointed.

Cruising back to the bay, he observes gulls gathered thick near the end of Hau headland, and steers in that direction. Then he anchors his launch, his curiosity caught, and rows his dinghy close into the rocks. The gulls flutter upward at his approach, like a pure white flag rippling and rising. Underneath, wedged in rocks, is what could have been Motu.

As his dinghy rises and falls in the swell, Frank looks at it and tries to make up his mind.

'Bloody thing,' he says finally. And he sees a flick of fin, and then the strong body arch again, high and bright out of the sea; he hears echo of his own laughter.

Perhaps I ought to forget finding this, he thinks, and leave them, back there, with their foolish wishes and wild fancies, with something.

For he has, one way and another, had his own.

In the end, though, he scrambles ashore, manages a rope around the reeking carcass, tows it back to the launch, and then home into the bay, the gulls swinging in confused cloud behind.